Belt Buckles
&
Pajamas

by
Michele LeBlanc

BELT BUCKLES & PAJAMAS

Copyright © 2007 Michele LeBlanc

All rights reserved.

* * *

Published by

KANAPOLIS FOG PUBLISHING EMPORIUM

Anderson, Indiana

FIRST PRINTING

ISBN-13: 978-0-6151-4714-7

ISBN-10: 0-615-14714-3

With Thanks to

Jessica, Amy, Brian, Mary

and Special Appreciation

to Chris Baty

One: In Which We Meet Some People

The doctor comes in. She's pretty. She looks friendly. I hope she isn't mean. Some of the others look mean to me. They scare me.

"Well, good morning everyone," the doctor says. "Let's all introduce ourselves. I'll start – my name is Andie. Now, who wants to go next?"

No one speaks. We all look at each other, around the stark white meeting room, at the floor, anywhere but her. Stuart starts to giggle. Theodore won't meet anyone's eyes. Glen is looking out for trouble. I know Violet is going to say something soon, if no one else does. She always wants attention.

"Well, isn't Andie such a sweet name. I think we could have some fun, Andie girl, once we get to, you know, know each other, if you know what I mean."

Violet is a whore. She thinks everyone wants her. She's right.

"Well, I do want to know you, but it would help if you told me your name."

Violet leans close into the doctor's face. Almost kissing her, she breathes out her name in that musky-throated way that turns people on. "Violet." She pulls back, smiling at how the doctor is embarrassed, how the doctor is pushing her black-rimmed glasses back up the curve of her nose, how she managed to get under her skin within the first ten seconds she met her.

"Okay, thank you, Violet," she stammers out. "Who's next?"

Stuart giggles.

"Okay, you just volunteered, what's your name?"

"Don't you know already? I know you do, THEY know, why don't you?"

It's another THEY day for Stuart, I guess. I look around to see what set him off. Oh, there's a camera in the corner. The blinking red light taunts him, each on and off sequence a little wink of the eye of Big Brother: now I'm watching, now I'm not, on and off and on and off.

"Well, I'm here all by myself, I'm not THEM, I promise you that. I have a name, remember? I'm Andie. What can I call you?"

He glares at the camera. She takes his hand, drawing his eyes away from the spying lens and to her own. "Please, tell me your name."

"Stuart. You can call me Stuart. But that's all I'm going to tell you. Until I know you're real." He turns away, she accepts it – for now, I presume.

Theodore looks up, as if Stuart's acceptance cleared the way for his own. He usually doesn't talk to the doctors. Maybe he thinks Andie is pretty. I know I think she is. Not sexy, like Violet, but pretty. Like best friend next-door slumber party and talk about boys pretty. Or how I always thought that should be. Damn Melissa for ruining all of that.

"You're human," Theodore says, and I realize how right he is. Doctor Martin, our usual doctor, is anything but human, and I wonder how she ever came to work for someone like him. The contrast is almost enough to make me think she isn't human, but her presence is so overwhelmingly convincing that I push that thought back.

She takes Theodore's hand, just as she took Stuart's. I want her to take mine; I reach out, but she only sees Theodore's hand, and mine goes ungrasped.

"We're all human," she tells him. "Tell me who you are."

"I am the conduit," he replies. "I am the beacon, I am the source. The contagion will spread through me, until there is no one left. We are doomed, this fragile race, this blight upon a wrecked orb twirling through the cosmos. And it shall come to pass, that the spore will cough its microbes upon the prevalent wind, and none shall escape and all will be one. There will be harmony throughout the universe, when the seed shall have a common strain and all the bastard off shoots have been shorn from this realm. The mighty, the weak, the good and the bad, there shall be no distinction when the wheat is reaped, when the land is raped, when the children are culled."

She continues to hold his hand, looking at him not with comprehension but with compassion. I can feel his heart beating, gone rapid during his tirade. It slows down as she continues to sit there, holding his hand. The fire leaves his eyes, his breathing no longer echoes in my ears.

"So, what's your name?" she asks again.

He stares at her.

"Well, I can't go on calling you 'Mister Conduit Beacon Source' and all that, can I?" she asks, her eyes twinkling, the corners of her mouth curling up in an oh so sweet smile. He is hers, that quickly, as "Theodore, I am the human Theodore," leaves his lips. There is only Glen left, now. Surely Glen will be my rock.

She looks at me now. She notices when I pull my hand back, still extended from when I listened to Theodore's rant. She notices, but does not judge. Her face remains impassive yet angelic. She smiles, my heart melts, and I wonder how long it will be before I am crying on her shoulder.

"Stop." Glen! Thank you!

She actually seems surprised at the authority in Glen's voice, at how his simple command causes her outstretched arm to cease its movement toward me in an instant, obeying despite any of her own intentions.

"You must leave her alone," Glen continues. "She must not be harmed." Bless him, God bless him.

Andie looks at me, looks at Glen. "I'm not here to harm anyone; I just want to get to know everyone."

"You can't know her," Glen tells her. "Not until she says it's okay. I won't let you. She is to be safeguarded from intrusion."

"Okay, so can I know you?" she asks him. "Is that all right?"

Glen ponders this. I can tell he is actually considering whether it would hurt me for her to know him. What a sweetie!

"Yes, I suppose that would be acceptable. Perhaps if you knew me, you would realize that she is safe, and that you need not interfere with her protection." He stands up, puts his arm across the solar system pattern emblazoned on his t-shirt. Okay, he's a sweetie, but sometimes he is a bit, well, dramatic. "I am The Guardian! Defender, Protector, Shield of my lady. I am The Guardian!" He kneels in his silly Guardian salute to me, and I hide my face. I can feel my ears burning red. He knows I don't like the salute, I tell him to stop but he won't.

He looks up at Andie. "But you can call me Glen, if you want to." Hmmph. Maybe he likes her too? What the hell is going on here?

Andie smiles at him, "Thanks — I think it would be a little easier if I did." She turns to me, again. I pull my legs up, resting my feet on the front of my chair seat, hiding my face in between my knees. Some protector Glen turned out to be, she is back at me already. Barely a minute's respite he gained me.

"Anyone else ready?" she asks, looking at me, knowing I'm the only one who hasn't gone yet. She was so nice earlier, when I was just watching and listening, and I want to talk to her, but I keep my face down, where she can't pull me out with those soft brown eyes that speak of walks in the woods and drinking wine by the fireplace and sharing a dog who smells when he gets wet but loves you no matter how many times you push him out of the bed.

"Daphne?" she asks, and I feel her pulling me up, lifting my head with those warm hands that aren't made of steel, that don't strike with the flat making the noise that echoes in my sleep.

I scream "No!" Before the word has left my mouth Glen has shoved her away from me. She tumbles into one of the folding chairs and it hits the carpeted floor with a soft clang. Sam the orderly has his knee in Glen's back before the sound has faded, twisting Glen's arms behind him; Glen is crying as Sam injects the tranquilizer. Andie is staring at me. I try to tell her that it isn't Glen's fault, but nothing comes out.

Two: An Encounter With Stuart

We are walking in the woods behind the dorm. Stuart is insisting that I go with him. I don't really like Stuart, but no one else does either, so I go along.

"I can't believe they thought they could get away with this," he says, agitated more than usual. "It's like they think I'm stupid!" He stops. "Do you think I'm stupid, Daphne?"

I look at him, not sure of what I think of him. It is getting colder; the sun has almost set. I decide ignoring the question would be best. "We need to get going," I tell him. "They'll notice if we don't make it back in time for supper."

He accepts the redirection easily enough and leads on. We go past the first line of trees and come into a small clearing. There are a couple dozen gravestones surrounded by a broken down fence.

"See? I told you it was here!"

I kneel by one of the stones. The markings are faded, but I can make out what was chiseled there: "# 37-433" on the top line, "07/04/1956" on the line below it. No name, just a number and a single date.

"The bastards think they can just ERASE US!" he shouts. "That we DON'T MATTER!"

"Maybe they didn't know?" I suggest timidly, without much belief in the idea or in swaying Stuart to believing it.

"Didn't know?" he asks incredulously. "Sure, maybe there are a couple people here that they weren't sure of when they were born, but EVERYBODY? And even if they all came in as John and Jane Doe, couldn't they have put whatever name they called them on there? Couldn't they have given them a little dignity?"

I have no answer for him. For once in his freaked out conspiracy laden life Stuart is right.

"I tell you," he continues, "this is where we all end up. Once they are done with the experiments, anyway. Once they have everything they want sucked out of our brains."

Okay, maybe he isn't completely right.

"We better get back."

We didn't talk on the return trip. Stuart was too busy thinking about the cemetery; I was worried about getting caught outside again. I didn't want to get put back on notice, there's no one to talk to when you are alone, no one to understand. No one to watch who's more messed up than you.

We make it okay. Sam wasn't around. Kareem – by far our favorite orderly in this place — might have seen us but he is always cool, as long as we don't cause any trouble. And we don't. Until supper, anyway, when Stuart starts screaming about being buried alive and that he will never, ever be number three seven dash four three three. It takes both Sam and Kareem to hold him down and tranq him up and then it's quiet again.

Three: Violet Is A Whore

I am sleeping. Sleep is real scary at first, but when you wake up and it's morning then you realize sleep is the best thing that was ever created. Once you are awake then you can forget about the part about having to lie there and try to fall asleep because you need to fall asleep to make it to the morning. If you don't make it to the morning it is your fault for not falling asleep.

The door opens and I keep my eyes shut. Sleep, sleep, sleep. I chant the words, hoping their spell will take hold. Go to sleep, I tell myself. Make it to the morning. It is your fault if you are not asleep.

He stands in the darkness. I keep the blinds shut tight because I don't want to see him; if I see him it means I am awake. I hear the belt buckle as it hits the floor. The sheets are pulled back. The cool air caresses my bare legs softer than any lover's kiss could. I keep my eyes squeezed tight as he lies down next to me. Hands pull down my panties, fingers poke inside of me, and it begins again. I am crying, but he only whispers words of love. His hand muffles my screams as he enters me.

I am awake. Violet holds me as I sob against her breast. She is not supposed to be here, we are supposed to sleep alone.

"There, there," she coos, stroking my hair. "It's okay, it was just a nightmare. I'm here with you, Daphne. I'm here with you."

She'll sleep with anyone. Even someone messed up like me. She's a whore. I love her.

Her caresses turn from comfort to need. She guides my hands between her legs. We cling to each other. Eventually, we sleep.

Four: More Than Just A Name

"Okay, good to see everyone again this morning." Andie is smiling, pretending that Glen didn't attack her, that she still likes us all, that today will be better than yesterday. They always pretend that last one, sometimes enough so I think maybe they actually believe it. After a while, though, they quit. On us. On themselves. On believing. They always quit.

She smells like coffee today. It is a good smell. A morning after everything is going to be okay and last night didn't happen and we woke up so we slept so nothing happened we were asleep none of it was our fault smell. And Mom would have bacon and eggs and Dad would pat her on the ass when she was cooking and she would laugh and everyone would love each other again. And if I cried Mom would keep cooking even if the eggs were burning and Dad would read the paper until I stopped.

"I'm sorry."

I look up from the smell and Glen is shy and how can he protect me from her if he is infatuated with her? If he sees her eyes and not mine when he closes his own?

"It's okay, Glen," she says in that soft silhouette of a voice that pulls me to her so much that I almost want Glen to release me from his guardianship, to drop the barrier separating me from Andie. "I know you were just looking out for Daphne. What you have to understand is that I am here to help her. I'm on your side, Glen, we both want what's best for Daphne. Let me help you protect her – don't you think she'd be safer with both of us looking after her?"

"Perhaps you are correct." He stands up, arm across the solar system. Sam moves closer, but Andie halts him with an open palm. Wow! The man-mountain Sam stopped in his tracks with a simple gesture by the lovely doctor – there are more levels to this woman than I can fathom. Glen continues his Guardian salute, dropping to his knees, face down, eyes closed, and shooting out his arm in an upright rocket blasting emulation. "Welcome to the Guardianship, Lady Andie."

"Thank you, Glen. I am honored."

Glen peeks up from his salute. He clears his throat and waits. Andie looks at him, confused. He clears his throat more loudly. Stuart giggles.

"Oh, I'm sorry, of course," she says, before dropping to her own knees and copying his salute.

"While you're down there, honey…" Violet says, her leer making her intent quite clear. I flush red – from embarrassment or jealousy I could not say.

Andie returns to her chair, a little flushed herself. "Violet, did you have something you wanted to talk about today?" she asks. Great, open the door a little wider why don't you – as if Violet needed an invitation to enter anywhere.

"Actually, I was a little curious about something," Violet says, leaning close to Andie. She brushes Andie's hair back over her ears, her hand trailing back to rest under Andie's chin. I see the goose bumps form on Andie's arm as she struggles to hold Violet's gaze.

"About what?" she asks.

"How you taste," Violet answers, lifting Andie's chin up and planting a kiss on the doctor's mouth. "Hmmm, sweet. And coffee." She laughs and sits down again, Andie watches her, trying not to show anything but I see the goose bumps, and I think she is looking a little more nipple-ly than the room temperature calls for. I think I am too, to be truthful.

"Violet, I appreciate your curiosity, but you cannot just kiss someone without permission. It isn't right to force yourself on someone else."

"Cannot? Like hell, it happens all the time. As for right or wrong, since when did that matter?"

"I understand that there are people who force themselves on others, and people who do not do what is right, but that doesn't mean we should be those kind of people. The only way things change, the only way we get better, is to make the proper choices ourselves. To respect other people. To do the right thing."

"Are you saying you didn't like it?" Violet asks in her best Bette Davis rasp.

"That's not the point; I'm saying you can't just do it because you want to!"

"Hmmph. Doesn't sound like you're saying you didn't like it."

Sam laughs. Andie shoots him a glare and he pretends to look out the window. Stuart giggles.

"So, you think that's amusing, do you?" she asks, but she smiles as she says it so we can tell she isn't going to yell. I hate it when they yell. Too many echoes with yells.

Stuart sits up straight. "It was funny, but scary too."

"How was it scary, Stuart?" she asks.

"Because when you talked to Violet you never answered her question and you spun it around and around just like THEY would."

"I'm sorry, Stuart, I never meant to ignore her question. And don't worry, I am not here to spin things, I am not THEM, I will be honest with all of you. I just want to help us all to get to know more about each other."

"I am not a number. I will never be number three seven dash four three three."

"Of course you're not a number, Stuart, you're a human being, and I know that. I accept you, Stuart."

Stuart is trying not to cry. He is clenching his fists and biting his lower lip. He loses the fight rather quickly. I watch as he sobs onto her shoulder, where I want to cry, and again I am jealous. How come they can reach out to her so easily?

She dries his eyes with the sleeve of her blouse. He tries to blow his nose on her sleeve but she is too quick and pulls it away. She motions for a tissue from Sam and lets him use that instead. No, not quite perfect, I guess. If she were perfect she would have had a handkerchief. Mary Poppins would have had a handkerchief.

"Now, what's this about number three seven four three three?" she asks.

"Dash. It's number three seven dash four three three. It's what I will never be. I will kill myself before I am number three seven dash four three three."

The room goes quiet. Sam is on the alert, ready to pounce. We hold our breaths as Andie takes this in. I can't believe he said it. He knows he can't say it. It's straight to being on notice, no chance for parole, go directly to jail, do not pass go, no $200, no nothing.

"Sam," she says, and I can see the word push through the air it is so thick.

"Ready, Doctor," Sam replies, preparing the tranq.

But then the world changes.

"Sam, please step outside for a second."

And we are breathing again.

"Excuse me, Doctor? Didn't you hear?" Sam is as baffled as the rest of us at this unprecedented turn of events.

"Now." There is no indecision in Andie's tone.

Sam's face, moments ago alive with the prospect of playing the heavy, falls as suddenly as ours rise. "Yes, Doctor. I'll be right outside, shout if you need me."

"And Sam?"

"Yes?"

Andie's face is stern as she looks at him. "You did NOT hear anything, understand?"

"Yes, Doctor," Sam replies. He leaves, slamming the door behind him.

We stare at Andie. This is a thing new to us. We wait to find out if it is salvation or damnation that is visiting our lives on this day.

Andie gets up and paces the room, walking back and forth across the twelve foot by twelve foot square. Her footsteps are barely audible as they fall on the beige carpet. We remain sitting, alternately staring at her and at Stuart. Stuart is trembling, just now realizing the enormity of what is occurring. At the words he had let slip out.

Glen saves Stuart – saves us all, really. Andie is turning from her to and fro, about to return on the fro, when he hits the floor and performs his Guardian salute in as smooth a rocket blasting motion as I have ever seen from him. "My lady Andie, we salute you." She stops in her tracks, about to reply, when he stands up, arm crossed over the solar system on his t-shirt.

"We salute the courageous stand against injustice you have taken on this momentous day," he continues. "We salute the solidarity you have shown. We salute the understanding, the compassion, the PROTECTION, you have bequeathed upon this sorry group." Glen stands still, arm brandished over solar system, awaiting acceptance.

Andie smiles, and we know it will be okay. Glen sits down. Andie comes over and leans over Stuart, who is still trembling. "It's okay, I know you're scared, but I promise – I swear – you will never be a number to me. Not three seven dash four three three, not forty-seven, not sixty-two million, not any number. You will always be a person."

She takes his head in her hands, and stares him straight in the eyes. Her face goes from mother to supreme monarch in a split second. "But you must NEVER EVER say you will kill yourself again, understand? Not in jest, not in anger, not to make a point – NEVER. If you ever do it again, I will not be able to stop them."

Stuart doesn't hold back the tears, but it's okay: they are tears of happiness, not fear or sorrow. "I won't, I swear I won't."

Five: *Theodore And Daphne Share A Dream*

There are bright lights all around. I can't tell where they are coming from – it is like the floor and the walls and the ceiling are all made of light. Theodore and I are lying on a flat table. There are several – well, not people, creatures? – around us, but I can't really see them. It is too bright, and my head feels funny.

"They're from outer space, you know," Theodore tells me, except I don't hear him with my ears – he is inside my head. It's like he knows what I am thinking. That scares me more than the creatures.

"They hooked our brains together," he tells me, again inside my head and not through my ears. He pushes a picture at me, an image coming to my mind unbidden, of us lying on the tables with wires going from his cut open scalp to a machine and more wires going to my own exposed brain.

"Get out of my head," I tell him, but it is no use, there is no off switch.

"I'm sorry," he says, trying not to think at me, but he does and it hurts. It hurts to see inside someone else and know what they think of you and know that they know what you think of them. To be naked and exposed. I want to sleep; I want it not to be my fault. I want to be alone inside but not outside my mind.

I try not to think of Theodore, I try not to hear his thoughts of me. To know he wants me. To think maybe I want him. That he knows what I am thinking.

"What do they want?" I ask. Not that I care, but it is something else to talk – to think – about.

He knows as soon as I ask that that is not what I am asking. But he answers anyway.

"They are coming. They are coming through me, the beacon, the source, the guide. They will infest the host organism and the virus will be cast out upon the masses and we will all die. They will absorb all that we are and we will be no more. They are different, so different from us, and we will never adjust to their ways. Their society. Their mores."

His mind throws at me more than just his diatribe, more than just images of this alien infestation overrunning our world. It is an onslaught of unnaturalness, of vivid scenes in more than three dimensions, and my head nearly explodes before saving darkness overtakes it.

"Were you there?" Theodore asks me at breakfast. "Do you remember?"

I stare at him with hatred until Glen tells him to leave me alone.

Six: *The Cemetery Revisited*

After breakfast they insist on dragging me out to the cemetery again. Stuart wants to show the headstones to everyone else.

"Now what do you say?" he says, triumphantly showing off the site. "Didn't I tell you?"

Theodore pores over each of the gravestones. "You're right, all numbers and dates, no names. Most disturbing." He looks at me and I turn away.

"I need everyone to promise something."

We look at Stuart, not thrilled at the idea of another promise you won't turn the lights off with your left hand because that's the direction of the gravitational flow of the government's neuromancer tracking force. Or swear to never start a sentence with the word ostrich because it resonates the hidden tuning forks and they can hear everything you say then. "Please," he says, "please promise."

"What is it?" I ask.

"When they get me – when they bury me out here – give me my name back. Find a chisel, a hammer, scratch it out with a rusty nail, anyway you can, please give me my name back. Don't let them make me a number."

Glen steps up to the plate. "The Guardian so promises."

Violet licks her lips. "Okay, baby, but you'll owe me something sweet later on."

"They won't get you, Stuart," Theodore says. "The alien host will have absorbed you and all you are far before that will happen."

"Theodore," Glen says with his humor him or else, guardianship wonderful self.

"Fine, I promise."

I hug Stuart. "She promised you would always be someone, Stuart. Andie promised."

He looks at me. "I know, but I need to know it from you, too, Daphne. I need to know I'll always be a name to you. I need that from you most of all."

I cry. He is so special. "Always, Stuart."

Seven: In Which The Bad Doctor Joins

The Good Doctor

We walk into our group session in the afternoon and everything sucks again. I should have known that it was a trap, that Andie wasn't for real, that nothing was changed and it would always, always, always suck.

"Gerard will be joining us today," Andie announces, as if we hadn't seen the evil emperor sitting there beside her. Gee, no kidding, that dark cloud of doom didn't give it away at all. Or the walls crushing in at one hundred miles per hour, encapsulating us once again in a friggin' prison. Just when the butterflies started to emerge out of the cocoons. Glen was even trusting her – he gave her the salute, inducted her into his little Guardianship club!

Doctor Martin – I guess his first name is Gerard, he never told us that – dismisses the introduction with a wave of his sweaty hand. "We've met, Doctor MacPherson." He turns to her, his expression as bothered while looking at her as it is when giving us the once over. "And please, it's Doctor Martin when we're with the patients." I couldn't see calling him Gerard anyway; Andie is okay, she's a first name person, but Doctor Martin will always be his title, not a real name, not a human being.

"Well it's still Andie, Doctor Martin." She turned her nose up on him! I've never seen anyone actually do that. Hmmph. Maybe she isn't in this by choice. He is the evil emperor, after all.

"I prefer to maintain an appropriate, professional distance – however, unless it interferes with patient care, you may have it as you wish. Let's get started, shall we?"

"Fine. Okay, so, who wants to start us off?"

Like that is going to work with Doctor Martin there. Stuart, despite himself, giggles.

"Do you find that amusing?" Doctor Martin asks.

"I'm not talking to you," Stuart replies. "You're with THEM. You probably assign the numbers, don't you?" He stands up, working up to a good old-fashioned Stuart tirade. "You probably chisel the numbers in with your fingers, don't you?" he shouts in the doctor's face. Sam pulls him back down to his chair. Sam is always a lot closer to us when Doctor Martin is here. I think Sam knows it is mostly the doctor's fault, because he only pulls Stuart back, he doesn't shove him down like usual.

"Still paranoid about them, are we Stuart?" Doctor Martin asks. He didn't even blink when Stuart got in his face, he just calmly took off his spectacles – other people have glasses, I think he has spectacles, kind of Ben Franklin like – and wiped them on his handkerchief. I guess I was wrong; Andie wouldn't have been perfect with a handkerchief, not if he uses one. She's better than I thought. She even knows what not to have.

"We're working on that," Andie interjects. "He knows that there are people who aren't after him; that's the first step."

"Oh, are there?" Doctor Martin asks. "Do you agree, Stuart? Is everybody out to get you or not?"

Stuart looks at Andie. She smiles, her warmth eclipsing the iceberg jutting from Doctor Martin's false concern.

"Oh, I see, can we be any more obvious? Doctor MacPherson, patient attachment is NOT a cure."

"It's not –"

"Oh please, spare me. If you cannot admit that, then I think we are done here."

"Okay, so what? It is still a beginning. It's still Stuart opening up, trusting someone."

Violet leans over and grabs Doctor Martin's crotch. "Hey Doc, you don't have a problem with a little intimate therapy, do you?" Trust Violet to act up when the attention isn't focused on her.

"Violet! Stop that!" Andie says. Sam tries to pull Violet back, but she holds firmly onto Doctor Martin's privates.

"Ow!" he shouts. "Let go, let go!" I'm not sure if he is talking to Sam or Violet, because it looks like there is a little action going on down there. Or rather response to Violet's action, as her mouth is now pressed against the front of his pants and her hands hold tight on either side of his fly. Doctor Martin tries to get away, and the chair flies out from under him. Violet lands on top of him, head still buried in his crotch, but her grip is broken by the fall and Sam succeeds in pulling her off of the doctor.

Doctor Martin gets up, and it is pretty apparent that at least the little doctor wasn't against some intimate therapy. He picks up his clipboard, holding it in front of him, his face turning beet red. "That's it! No more of this coddling best friend bullshit – I am administering the treatment this afternoon. Sam, keep her in isolation until then."

He storms out. Violet tries to turn and kiss Sam, but he holds her tight. Andie sighs.

"But Andie, darling –," Violet tries to wheedle her way out of the situation, but Andie cuts her off.

"Sorry, he's head of staff, and that was – well, it was too much, Violet. I can't stop it. Maybe, maybe it will help." She turns away.

"It's okay, Violet, I will do it for you," Glen offers. "I can handle it."

Sam smirks. "Sure you can. It'll be real fun, when the first jolt hits you."

Eight: Bolts Of Lightning

It must be a dream because Glen is flying. Really up in the air, no strings attached, cape flapping behind him flying. And his t-shirt has somehow become this really geeky comic book superhero costume. I can still tell it's him because he isn't wearing a mask.

Anyway, there he is. Flying. He smiles at me, waves, and flies down to land next to me. "I am glad you called me, Daphne."

"I called you?"

"Well of course. This is a job for The Guardian, after all."

I am so confused. I hate it when I don't know what is going on in my dream. Wait a minute. I guess it is worse when I do know what is going on. Because it is always what it shouldn't be. What isn't right. Glen is waiting for me to speak. I just look at him, not knowing what to say.

He clears his throat. Oh, I get it. "Yes, of course, Guardian. Do your job. Save us all."

"Thank you my lady. I vow to stop this tempest that has beset us, to root out the source of the maelstrom that threatens our very existence, to quell the –"

"Glen. Guardian. Just do it, please?" I ask, not able to absorb anymore of his analogies or metaphors or whatever the hell he is spouting at me.

He salutes me, and flies up into what I now see as a very unhappy sky. Funny how that can just suddenly change like that, how it can turn from blue sky with puffy clouds to dark grey thunderheads in an instant. Surely I should have noticed all those bolts of lightning and huge hailstones and funnel shaped clouds of eerie green before this. But I think he was in a blue sky when he flew down to me, I am almost sure the sky had been blue.

So off he goes and stuff is hitting him and he fights against the swirling winds. There are lots of flashes of lightning and then I realize what is happening. He is losing. Glen is losing. The Guardian is losing. My protector is losing. He gets hit by a huge lightning strike and starts falling, his silly cape wrapping around him like a shroud, his limbs flapping aimlessly as he plummets to his death.

He strikes the ground and the sound is louder than all the thunder of the storm raging around us. "No!" I scream, running to where he lays prone on the ground. I kneel by him, head on my lap, urging him back, pleading for him not to leave me.

I look up as the lightning strikes nearby, I smell the ozone, I feel the static charge. The next bolt is for me, I know it is. "Glen, help me!" I scream at him, shaking him.

He stirs. "Daphne, my lady. I am sorry, I have failed."

"Help me!" I shout again.

"My lady!" he cries, with a final gasp, and then shoves me out of the way as the bolt strikes him full in the chest.

I get up, looking up at the storm, swearing at it, cursing it for taking my protector. "Come on," I scream. "I will rip you apart," I threaten. "I have his strength now; he will shield me always, whether or not you have killed him! I am NOT helpless!"

And just as suddenly as it struck the storm subsides, and I am left with Glen's lifeless body, and I hold it and cry over it until once again darkness comes and I sleep.

Nine: In Memoriam Of A Hero

"He saved me," I tell the others. We are at the cemetery, looking for his grave. "The least we can do" – Stuart nods at this, knowing what I must say – "is mark his grave."

Theodore looks at me. "So, you were in a dream with him when this happened? Like we were?"

"No! Okay, yes, damn it, I admit it, I remember that dream with you and the aliens." I need them to believe me about what happened to Glen, and I think they do, but God I don't want to remember Theodore's dream. I don't want him to know what I am inside, like he knew in the dream. I start crying. That always gets him off my back.

"Geez, Theodore," Violet says, "cut her a break. Her great big strong hero just bit the big one on her and here you are talking about the wet dreams you shared with her."

"They weren't wet dreams, Violet," Theodore says, embarrassed.

"Too bad, because let me tell you, she's fun when you get her going, aren't you sweetie?" Violet brushes my lips with her fingertips. I keep crying – it's all I have against them, I can only hope it works.

Stuart is rustling among the gravestones. "I don't think he's here. I checked all the numbers. None of them are new."

I stop crying. "He's got to be here! Where else would they bury him?"

Theodore looks straight up. "Maybe they took him."

"THEY?" Stuart asks, panicking.

"Not YOUR they, idiot. The aliens. The ones in the ship," he explains, pointing up at the sky.

I look up. Clouds in the background, framed by a latticework of bare branches, most of their leaves already littering the grass around us. "We have to get him back, then," I say. "It's not right; he doesn't deserve to be dissected by some alien creatures."

Theodore shakes his head. "None of us do, but what are you going to do?"

"We're going after him."

"What do you mean?"

I look at him, and suddenly don't hate the little creep. "You're the beacon, the source, the meaning of life and all that, right? So we're going to dreamland together again, Theodore. The Guardian deserves a proper resting place, and we're going to make sure he gets it."

Violet kisses number three seven dash four three three. "Just in case," she says. Stuart giggles.

Ten: Andie Gets All Professional

We are all sitting in group again. At least all doesn't include Doctor Martin this time. Sigh. It also doesn't include Glen.

"Okay, who's first?" she asks for it seems the millionth time. "Come on, someone has to start and it isn't going to be me today."

Violet sneers at her. "It sure isn't going to be Glen either."

"Shut up," I tell her.

Andie looks at me. "Daphne? You want to talk about it?"

I glare at Violet, mad she made me speak out loud. Andie keeps looking at me. I want to tell her about Glen, how he saved me, how I need her now since he is gone. But then I think about Glen taking that last bolt, sacrificing himself for me, and how those bastard alien creatures have sucked his body into some celestial void that only Theodore and I can retrieve it from and I decide maybe I better not. "No."

"Are you sure, because if not, it sounds like Violet can share something with us."

Violet smiles, licks her lips, "I can share all kinds of things, Andie dear."

"No!" I won't let Violet turn Glen's death into another excuse to show off. "It's –" I pause, not wanting to discuss it, but knowing there is no way to hide it. I bite my lower lip and decide maybe a little bit of truth will get me through. "Well obviously Glen is gone. But I can't tell you where. I'm going to bring him back."

Andie smiles tenderly. "Daphne, you don't have –"

"It's okay, I know I don't need him. I'm not HELPLESS anymore. But I owe it to him, to give him a proper burial. To give him my last regards. He was a hero, you know."

"I know he was, Daphne. And it sounds like you are doing right by him. Just let me know if I can help – while you aren't helpless, that doesn't mean you have to do everything alone."

Theodore pipes in, surprisingly cheerful. "It's okay, Andie. I'll be with her."

Stuart giggles.

"That should be a riot," Violet offers. "A regular freak show."

"Shut up," I tell Violet for the second time ever. She looks hurt. I've never hurt her before – she's probably faking. Surely I don't have the power to crack her indomitable spirit.

Andie looks at Violet. "Violet, I think we need to have a serious discussion."

"I don't do serious."

"I mean it. What happened with Doctor Martin, well, we just can't have a repeat of that. Don't you understand? He'll order you to undergo further treatments and I won't be able to stop him."

"I kind of liked it," Violet purrs in response. "It felt... tingly. Sort of like a super charged vibrator. I think I came five times."

"Another dose and you won't feel anything. No tingles, no cumming, no nothing. You have to behave yourself around him. If you cross him again, if you force him to administer additional treatments, well I'm afraid I won't be able to reach you again."

"Oh Andie, I knew you liked me, I just knew it! Now, how about we kiss and make up?" Violet leans in close to Andie, her lips slightly parted, exhaling her warm breath on the doctor's pearly white skin.

"Stop it!" Andie says, pushing Violet back. Sam steps closer, but Andie waves him away. I can tell he is disappointed; he liked it when he had to pull Violet off of Doctor Martin. I think he copped a feel.

Violet pouts. "Was it something I said?"

Andie glares. "Violet, we have talked about this. I am being completely candid. You have to respect other people's personal space. Just as other people have to respect yours. It's a two way street, but you have to cooperate. No more throwing yourself at people. No more grabbing. No more uninvited kissing. Actually, no more kissing, invited or not. Not while you are here."

"Not even little butterfly kisses?" she asks, and I can't help but laugh. Stuart giggles, even Theodore smiles. Andie doesn't.

"No."

Violet sits back, arms crossed, little schoolgirl forbidden to play. "Fine."

"I mean it."

"I know, I know. Lay off already."

Eleven: The Search For Glen

Sleep, sleep, sleep. If I can go to sleep then I can go with Theodore and find Glen. Sleep, sleep, sleep, I repeat the mantra. It's weird, trying to fall asleep with Theodore instead of Violet. She's so soft and clingy and comfy and he's – well, he's not any of that. I'm worried that Sam or Kareem will find us out but Violet promised she would take care of us, that we wouldn't be discovered. I knew she cared about me, I'm sorry I hurt her at group today.

"Be quiet, Daphne, I can't think if you are that loud in my head," Theodore tells me, but it is with my mind that I hear him and I know we crossed over into the dream world.

"Sorry, Theodore, but you know we made it, don't you?"

"Oh, I guess we did. Okay what now?" he asks.

"What the hell do you mean what now? You're the beacon, these are your friggin' aliens, why are you asking me?"

"Ouch!"

"Sorry I forgot. I didn't mean to attack like that. I just forget that we are linked and you are hearing all this," and then my apology turns too loud as the circular pattern of my thinking about what Theodore is hearing me think escalates and I can't help but thinking at him, "Stop! I don't want you in my head. Get out! Get out! Get out!"

Theodore reels away, I feel our connection fading; he is almost gone when I call him back. "Theodore, please, I'm sorry, please I need you."

"Really?" he asks in his little boy voice. "I thought you wanted me out." Grrrr, he can be such a baby. "I heard that."

"Come on, I just can't handle too much, okay? I do need you, you have to help me find Glen, I can't do it without you."

His relief, his acceptance pours over me, threatening to push me out, to drown me. "Control, Theodore," I plead. I have to have control I tell him. He pulls back only a little this time, so we are linked but not submerged within each other, so I can at least pretend that he isn't privy to every little thought I have about Glen about Stuart about Theodore about Violet about Andie.

Theodore calls out. To them. He activates his beaconness. I feel the tug of the otherworldly from him. The unnatural strangeness of being, the alien, the foreign, the outside. I hold onto all that I am, I latch onto the thought that there are others like me. Lovers like Violet. Angels like Andie. Heroes like Glen.

Theodore becomes a vortex, a black hole pulling in the universe around him. I am drawn to his center, to his strangeness, to alien incarnate, and disappear.

It is all bright again. The creatures surround me. I look for Theodore but he isn't with me. Oh God, Theodore where are you I can't be alone not with them not with these aliens!

Serenity washes over me. I feel calm, peace, love and acceptance. I recognize the feelings that had emanated from Theodore and I look around expectantly but he isn't there. The creatures move closer and I realize they are the source of these feelings and I try to push it away, try to reject them, but the essence that is Theodore refuses to let me.

I feel, rather than hear by mind or ears, what Theodore says to me: "Accept this union, Daphne, become one with us. You are not alone, you need never be alone. Be one with us, join this union."

"No!" I tell him – them. "I am not one of you, I will not be undone, I am ME! I am Daphne!"

"We are not aliens, Daphne. Look at us." I keep eyes closed, I try to shut out the voice but it is within me and cannot be silenced. "LOOK AT US!"

I am forced to open my eyes and the sight shocks me. Glen and Theodore are standing there – Glen, standing! – where the creatures had been. And Kareem and Andie and my third grade teacher and the guy who delivered our newspaper which Dad hid behind no don't think about that and Melissa is there and the President and the people from the bus stop and... and everybody. And they aren't creatures, they aren't aliens, they are people.

"That's what I'm saying," Theodore says, and all the rest of the people fade back to the now gray background. The bright light is gone, and Theodore is smiling – I don't know if I have ever seen him smile, but here he is smiling! "It's all good now, Daphne. I have been absorbed into the great wash of humanity, this divine continuum of which we are all a part. That is the great message, my lady," – (I knew he called me that because he was as much a part of Glen as he was of me now) – "that we are all together, regardless of our own solitude, irrespective of our loneliness, there is always the commonality of spirit with which we all have our part. The fabric of time is interwoven in your thread as well as all those you meet. Do not be afraid of the others, my lady, for they are you and you are they. Love them, and let them love you."

"But Glen –"

"Glen is fine, and the kiss Violet bestowed upon the marker of an unknown soul in the cemetery just as surely landed on his forehead. You have made your journey; you have paid your respects. Rest well, and wake knowing you are part of the greater whole, that there is no outside, that you are always inside the soul of the cosmos."

Then they all fade way, and I am left with a feeling of belonging. I close my eyes and I sleep. Without any scary dreams. Or scary real things.

Twelve: In Which No One Dies That We Know Of

The breakfast table is almost empty now. Me, Violet, Stuart. We can hardly sustain an argument with just three of us. Violet gets up, walks over to the table with the weirdoes. Good God, we aren't that desperate for amusement, are we?

"Hey, Shy Boy, what's up?" Violet leans over the poor sap. He doesn't have a chance. Thirty seconds later he is sitting with us, sipping his white milk and trying not to make eye contact. Violet is the only one who calls him Shy Boy. The rest of us really don't call him anything – he wouldn't answer even if we did. Rumor has it that he killed three people. Hard to believe, all he does here is sit and drool. I have never heard him say a word. I question whether he is going to improve the breakfast table conversation.

Pet Shop is next. His real name is Herbert but we all call him Pet Shop. He isn't very funny but the invisible talking animals that follow him everywhere are hilarious. Violet asked him once if they did any tricks, and if so she would like to borrow a couple for the night, but Pet Shop didn't get the joke. He also didn't let her borrow any of them. She got over it.

We still had one chair left but no one was willing to sit in that one. Damn Melissa. Even absent, she kept her claims.

Shy Boy has an old AM/FM radio with an earplug that he uses to listen to ball games. Stuart asks Shy Boy if he could hear anyone from the outside on it. Shy Boy clutches his radio tightly. That's as much of an answer as we get from him.

"Probably getting brainwashed right now," Stuart states. "You know they can transmit commands over FM radio waves. It's how they convinced people to use fluoride."

I lean over and look at the radio. Shy Boy didn't flinch, but he didn't offer me the earplug either. I saw it was on AM but decided to let Stuart figure that out on his own. I'm sure he has some other government mind control theory for AM.

Apparently, Pet Shop's menagerie has other thoughts on the matter. "Video killed the radio stars," one of them states loudly. Well, Pet Shop says it but it doesn't sound like him so we know it is one of his animals.

Stuart nods his assent.

"Ah, ya stupid hedgehog, what the 'ell do ya know about it, ya ignorant rodent." I guess the animals are not living in complete political harmony.

"The cow jumped over the moon."

"What?" exclaims Stuart, "there's been another launch? Damn them and their secret satellites. Come on, we only have a few hours to tin foil the showers."

Violet laughs. "See, Daphne, we can still have entertainment, even without the super hero and the Martian."

She gave a mischievous grin. "I might even get a peep out of Shy Boy."

I look to see why she thinks she can make him say anything and am well, not actually surprised or shocked, to see she has her leg stretched out under the table. She is rubbing her sole across the front of Shy Boy's pants. He sits there with a glazed look on his face, rocking back and forth with the motion of her foot.

"You better quit that, you know if you get caught you're in big trouble," I tell her. "Don't forget your promise to Andie."

"I didn't promise anything about not sticking my foot under the table. It's not my fault Shy Boy happens to be sitting there, is it? And anyway, look at the poor boy, he's in heaven."

I have to admit Shy Boy does look better than I have ever seen him. The earplug has slipped from its place; I can almost hear the tinny broadcast of the football game from where I am sitting. He must be nearly deaf to be playing it that loud. He sits and rocks against Violet's foot for a couple minutes before he lets loose in his pants. Violet smiles at him, pulls her foot back and leans across the table.

"I wanted to thank you for joining our table, Shy Boy. But it's got to stay our little secret okay? Can't tell anybody –

not Doctor Martin or Andie or Sam or anybody. Now go clean up and we will see you at lunch."

Shy Boy gets up and walks off toward the hallway that leads to the rooms.

"He didn't peep, but he sure did pop," I tell Violet.

She smiles. "Don't be jealous, love, we'll have time later, I promise."

"I'm not jealous. You're just going to get in trouble if you keep violating personal spaces. That's what Andie said."

Violet stares at me. I guess I hurt her again.

"Fine, if that's the way you want. Enjoy your nice cold bed."

"Violet, don't be that way."

She licks her lips. "Okay, sweetie, I was just teasing; you know I'll be there tonight. You know I'll always be there for you."

"Lean on me," intones the invisible hedgehog.

Thirteen: Group Therapy With The New Group

"I see we have some new faces today." Andie is such the friggin' student of the obvious. But she is so nice about it. And she smells like coffee again.

Violet takes over the conversation. She's been doing that a lot lately, ever since Glen... Well, since there's been no one to keep her in line.

"Well, I had to get somebody to fill up the space with Glen and Theodore off traipsing around in Never-Never land, didn't I?" she asks Andie. "I mean, God, we have to have something to talk about other than my libido and Stuart's conspiracies. So I invited Shy Boy and Pet Shop to give us some new topics of discussion."

Andie smiles at Violet's recruits. "Well, Herbert, how are you today?"

Pet Shop beams back at her. How could anyone not smile at her? God, she is so... NOT Doctor Martin.

"Sunshine on my shoulders makes me happy," the hedgehog offers. He has it right: Andie is just like stepping into a warm sunbeam that ignores the arctic breeze and shines through the living room window and you just want to curl on the floor and let its warmth soak through to the bone.

"I'll take that as you being okay with joining us today. How about you, Gordon?"

We all look around. "Who the hell's Gordon?" Stuart asks. "Is someone hiding? Is it one of THEM?"

Andie is looking at Shy Boy. "Hey, it's Shy Boy," Violet says. "Shy Boy has a name!"

Shy Boy looks over at Violet, not making eye contact, rather looking down at her feet. Violet grins. Andie sees the exchange. I know we are in trouble. Again.

"Violet, what exactly brought Gordon into this group?"

"Got me Andie, maybe he heard about the rave we were having later."

Andie isn't amused. She is even less amused when she sees the little tent Shy Boy is pitching. He rocks back and forth, still staring at Violet's feet. "Gordon," she says, "why don't you go on back to your room. You can join us again tomorrow, if you are feeling, um, better."

"Rocket man," the hedgehog says. We try not to laugh, but Stuart just can't help giggling sometimes.

Andie turns on Violet as soon as Gordon has left the room. "Violet," she says, her face almost red with anger, "if I find out you are abusing Gordon, if you are doing anything to that boy, this will all be over. No second chances, no excuses. Over. Am I clear?"

"Andie, I haven't laid a hand on Shy Boy. I swear." She says it with such a straight face, such sincerity; she would be a great actress. Or poker player. But I guess, in her own way she is telling the truth, it wasn't a hand. I think Andie suspects she isn't speaking the whole truth and nothing but the truth, but she lets it slide.

Andie takes a deep breath. You can almost see the halo coming back to rest. "Daphne, do you want to tell me what happened to Theodore?"

I look at her. I know she wants to know what really happened. I know she wants to figure this out. So do I. But I can't. That whole one with the cosmos Glen and Theodore and my third grade teacher and everybody else... it can't be real. How could I ever be one with everybody when everybody would have to include... *him*? If he was ever one with humanity, if he was ever any piece of good, how could he have...

"I need tin foil," Stuart says, to break the silence.

"Daphne," Andie tries again, "please talk to me. I just want to listen to what you have to say."

"The eye in the sky," says the hedgehog.

"SEE! I told you! It isn't just me, the hedgehog knows about it too." Stuart jumps up and Sam steps in. I'm starting to wonder why Sam is ever back far enough to have to step forward. I mean, geez, it's his job: you'd think he would know one of was going to flip out every session. But Stuart isn't going after Andie, he just wanted to stand up so he could wave his hands around and point up at the sky. No, not the sky, the ceiling – it would be the sky if we weren't inside. Sam backs away when he sees that Andie isn't in immediate danger from Stuart.

"THEY are watching us," he says, gesturing madly. "If we don't put up the tin foil, if we don't block their mind reading ultraviolet rays then we are doomed. DOOMED I say!"

"Mooooo," says, I believe, a cow from Pet Shop's herd. If it wasn't a cow that hedgehog is doing a damn fine impression of one.

"Yes, mooooo," Stuart agrees. "That's what tipped me off, the cow jumping over the moon." He gets real quiet, crouches down a little, and whispers, "They are using the moon to hide behind. That's where the satellite is."

Andie leans back, sighs heavily. Good, she has given up on me, I am safe.

"Stuart, just because Herbert brings up –"

"It's not Herbert," he breaks in. "It's the hedgehog. Those guys hear everything. They're the perfect spies. Who would suspect a hedgehog of eavesdropping?"

"Whoever you heard it from, I assure you there is not a satellite hiding behind the moon, bombarding us with ultraviolet rays that read our minds. It just isn't possible."

"It isn't?"

"No," she answers. "Ultraviolet rays have a maximum distance of three hundred miles before degrading, the moon is well over fifty thousand miles from us – it just wouldn't work, scientifically speaking." I have no idea what she is saying, or proving, but the way she says it – I would have believed anything she said then.

"Oh," Stuart says. He giggles – he almost sounds like a girl when he giggles, it is kind of cute – and sits back down. "Never mind."

"Mooooo," the cow assents.

Andie turns to me. I am still a little melted from how sweetly she had straightened Stuart out. I have never seen anyone calm him down like that, not so quickly, nor so effectively, and certainly never so lovingly.

"Theodore is gone." I can't help it. I have to tell her something. She deserves it.

"Yes," she replies. "Violet told me that much, now how about you tell me how it happened?"

I look at her, her soft brown hair, with little curls around the ears. Her pale, smooth skin, her pretty lips and white teeth and proportioned body and her so not Melissa everything. How could I ever be a part of that? How could Andie and... and *him* ever be a part of the same universe? I cry. But not on her shoulder. Not where I want to.

She tries to comfort me but Violet pushes her back – not so roughly that Sam comes after her, but firm enough to show Andie she isn't welcome, that it isn't her place to hold me, that Violet still... owns me? Is that what she thinks? I pull back from Violet, stop crying and dry my eyes on my sleeve.

"How can you exist?" I ask. "How can you be real?"

"Daphne, am I that unbelievable? I thought we were making contact, that you knew you could trust me." She doesn't get it. She doesn't realize just how much contact she has made. I shudder, thinking what she would find out if she ever shared a dream with me, if she ever linked minds with me as Theodore had. If she ever saw inside my thoughts.

She reaches out, and this time I don't pull back. I tremble as she places her hand on my arm. Violet wants me to push Andie away again, I can tell by her icy stare, but I don't want to. I let the hand sit there; I feel the warmth of her skin against my arm.

"Believe in me, Daphne. I believe in you."

My eyes brim with tears I believe in her so much. She squeezes my arm, and I can sense the pulses of light, the goodness, emanating from her, flowing into my own veins as pure as a transfusion of holy water.

"Glen is with Theodore. They are both gone, but it is okay. They are part of... part of everything now. Theodore tried to explain it to me but it was a little, well, metaphysical. Zen and all that."

"But they are in a good place?" she asks.

I try to think if it is good or evil or if it just is. I know what she wants the answer to be. "It's good," I tell her, but I don't think that is the complete truth. Because if you add in the good people with the bad people, if they are all part of it, then doesn't it just kind of wash out in the end? Even super goodness like hers has the equally evil counterpart. I know that. God how I know that.

"I'm glad," she says. "But what about you? Did Theodore tell you how you fit into this good place?"

"Sort of. He told me I was a part of it. That you were a part of it. Every – everyone was a part of it. That there weren't any aliens, that even though we are alien to each other we are still part of the same... humanity."

I can tell I hit a home run with that answer. Andie is glowing. I think the no aliens thing was really important for her to hear. I guess I'm glad I told her, if only to see her reaction. I might have to come up with some more stuff like that; it's worth it to see her radiate. To think that I can cause her to look like that, it makes me glow a little myself. And then it crashes as rapidly as it had been built. Just like always. Bastards.

"Are THEY a part of it?" Violet asks.

"Oh my God, that's how they absorb us!" Stuart shouts. "We have to figure out a blocking mechanism. Maybe a virus to reject the host organism? Tin foil won't work on an organic transformation, we're going to need a laboratory. Something with microscopes and test tubes and samples of alien DNA."

Andie's glow fades. Damn Violet. You knew that would happen. She just had to push the buttons, had to turn the spotlight back on her.

"We all live in a yellow submarine," says the hedgehog. No one is particularly amused.

Fourteen: Stuart Builds A Machine To Save Us All

We are back at the cemetery. Violet brought along her two new toys, Shy Boy and Pet Shop. I wonder if there are any animals buried here. Probably not, they never let us keep any pets. Not visible ones you have to feed, anyway.

Stuart found some tin foil. I think he got it from the kitchen. He just has the roll, not the box with the cutting edge on it. That's a good thing. He would most likely try injecting us with his anti government takeover serum if he could cut us open. I think I will stick with the meds they give us versus whatever botulism-inducing potion Stuart would cook up in the bathroom.

He is building little antennae and funky triangle shaped reflecting things. I don't even pretend to understand him when he tells us how they will refract the mind reading rays and distort the reception by the moon satellite.

"But I thought the moon was thousands of miles away," Pet Shop tells Stuart. I think he just wants to get out of climbing the tree. Stuart says the triangle reflectors have to be at least twenty feet high to be effective. I don't blame Pet Shop, I don't want to climb up there either. It doesn't look safe. Tree climbing is safe if you are a kid and in your own back yard but it's been a long time since that was true.

"Up on the roof," says the hedgehog.

"Exactly!" Stuart nods his head. "The flaw in Andie's logic is that she was relying on government statistics! Of course they are going to provide her with misinformation. Thank God we have the advantage of the hedgehog surveillance network or we would have fallen for it as well. You really can't blame her, for it was an impressive argument, with quite lovely presentation. I liked her sweater."

"I liked what was under the sweater," Violet says. Sometimes Violet isn't being crude, sometimes she just says what we all are thinking. We nod our heads in agreement with her –

except Shy Boy, of course. He just drools, but it is hard to tell if it is because of Violet's comment or just regular drooling.

Stuart points up the tree. "Okay, Pet Shop, up you go. Time's a-wasting, once the moon crests over Jupiter it will be too late to block the signals."

I hear Pet Shop muttering about his damn monkey never being around when he needs him. I thought that was kind of funny. Usually it's the animals he has that are funny, but that time it was Pet Shop himself with the good one.

While Pet Shop is in the tree we set up the tin foil antennae on branches we can reach from the ground all around the cemetery. We add some more to the broken down fence that is failing to keep out the weeds or us or probably anything that wants to broach the perimeter. It is going pretty good, we are almost out of tin foil, when we hear it.

"Screeeeeeech!"

Stuart hits the ground, eyes wide open, glancing around nervously. "Has the moon set over Jupiter? Somebody look, somebody tell me, has it started? Are they here?"

"Screeeeeech!" It echoes through the cemetery again.

Violet laughs. "Look up there, Pet Shop's got a new friend!" We get up, a little embarrassed when we see Pet Shop flapping his arms up in the tree. There is a big old owl on the branch next to him, flapping back. I swear to God it looks like they are talking.

"You go, Pet Shop," Violet calls to him. He smiles, flaps his arms, and lets out his own loud screech.

The owl must have felt we were intruding on a private conversation, because it took off after that. The wings are huge, but it barely makes a sound as it glides from the tree and through the woods. It was beautiful but it made me nervous, how quick and silent it was. And those claws and that beak. Anything that hunts in the night, when you are alone. Unaware. Scared.

"Come on, Shy Boy, I need a reverse transmitter to complete the anti government meta ray wave insaturation deflection device." Stuart pleads. He is trying to get Shy Boy's radio. Like that is going to happen. That thing is attached to him. The only time I ever saw him not pay any attention to it was when...

Violet must be in a good mood, if she is helping Stuart out. Or maybe she is just in her normal horny mood. Either way, she saunters – no one else saunters like Violet, let me tell you – up to Shy Boy. Stuart smiles; he knows Shy Boy doesn't stand a chance.

She smoothes his hair back with those sensuous hands. "Come on, Shy Boy, don't you want to help us out?" It is funny to see him try to pull back with his top half while his lower half tries to grind against Violet.

"Listen, sweetie," she coos, pulling the earplug out of his ear, blowing into it her hot, warm, musky breath that feels like the ocean and the sunset and a sauna. "How about we do a little trade? We just want to borrow it for a little while."

He stops pulling back, as she tugs on his pants. His hands hang limp by his side. As she takes him in her mouth, she unclips the radio from his belt loop. He doesn't notice. She could be cutting off his arm and he wouldn't notice.

Five minutes later, Stuart has his reverse transmitter, and the anti government meta ray wave insaturation deflection device is completed. Shy Boy – well he almost smiles at me. I sometimes wonder about Violet, but maybe this is good for him, despite what Andie said about invading personal spaces.

"We'll give it back in a couple days," Stuart tells Shy Boy. "Their satellite is so big it can only hide behind the full moon."

We head home. Halfway back we realize we forgot Pet Shop, and return to the cemetery. He is still screeching in the tree, looking for his owl friend. We convince him that the bird is gone and he reluctantly climbs down.

"We'll come back tomorrow, Pet Shop. We have to recalibrate the deflection device every night. Those government scientists aren't idiots, you know. They will change the frequency of wave transmission at least once a day. No resting on our laurels, or it is off to the empty mind draining vacuum of assimilation." Stuart is so encouraging when he wants to be.

Fifteen: Lunch Does Not Start Well

We found out where Stuart got the tin foil. For some reason, it had slipped all of our minds that today is the stupendously popular grill out day. The one day each year that the crazies get to look at real burning fires. And eat wonderful char-grilled hamburgers and burnt hot dogs and sometimes we get cut up potatoes (we don't get to cut them up, of course) and onions and peppers and wrap them in foil – tin foil, specifically – and throw them on the coals. Except we don't have any tin foil. It's all hanging around the cemetery, keeping us safe from government mind control waves. According to Stuart. He isn't even acting like he is sorry that we are all sitting on the grass near the grills and the picnic tables and not getting fed.

Sam is not in a happy state of mind. "If whoever stole the foil doesn't confess real soon there's going to be no burgers for anyone," he says. "I want my grilled potatoes and carrots, damn it!" I forgot about the carrots. Those are good too. Sam usually does all the cooking on grill out day; I think he is taking the missing foil very personally. Andie says we need to not take things personally, but when it is true how can you not?

Stuart is not giggling. Violet is not going for Sam's penis. Shy Boy, well, is remaining in character, so that isn't a problem. Even the hedgehog is silent. I don't know the last time we were able to keep a secret. I thought for sure Pet Shop would have given us up; we did leave him up in the tree, after all, but so far so good, all lips are sealed, no fingers pointing, no Benedicting Arnold.

Andie, the lady of the lake, the angel from above, arrives, in her faded jeans and casual sweatshirt that says rolling in the leaves and holding hands and singing off key old eighties songs at the bar on karaoke night. Andie arrives, and we all catch our breath. Stuart giggles, as he thinks the gig is up. I hold my faith, newly found, that it is in fact not quite up, not if I do, as I do, believe in Andie.

"What's the matter, Sam?" she asks, catching him off guard. How can anything be the matter when she is talking to you, when she is showing she cares? Sam is not immune to the wonder that is Andie, I have known that since I saw her halt him with a simple gesture.

"They took the tin foil, Doctor MacPherson. How can I cook my carrots without the tin foil?" He looks sad enough to cry. I think about running and getting a couple of the triangle reflectors off of the tree, but know Stuart would raise a fuss if I did.

"Now, Sam, we don't know that anyone took it, do we? Perhaps it was just misplaced. Or maybe someone borrowed it. I am sure if anyone borrowed it they will be more than happy to return it in time for you to cook your carrots. Why don't you go ahead and start the burgers and hot dogs and I will see if I can find you some foil, okay?"

She guides him back over to the grills. He gives us a dirty look, as if he knows despite what Andie said that no one misplaced or borrowed his tin foil, that he knows for certain that someone took it deliberately and that once he finds out who it was they are in trouble. And I think he is pretty sure he already knows who that someone is. But that doesn't really matter since Andie is successful in getting him started on the burgers and hot dogs and even better she comes over to us after Sam is handled and sits on the grass next to us and I want to cry. Not because of sadness or missing foil or no potatoes but because it is so right having her next to me on the grass, not asking me questions or worrying about what I was dreaming or giving me another pill but just being there. Next to me. No strings attached.

Kareem asks us if we want to play catch with his football. I think he is really asking Violet but has to include us to be polite. We are all happy sitting there. Violet tells Pet Shop to play with Kareem, I think she likes watching the boys run around. Shy Boy even goes out there. He isn't catching the ball or throwing the ball or running around with the ball. But he is out there. The fresh air is good for him, I think. He is looking less of a weirdo now. He brushes his hair now before coming to group. And his teeth, too. He might have a crush on Violet. Violet laughs when I tell her this, says he's missing the boat, that she's all about me. It's hard to believe her when she keeps grabbing guys by the penis but she says she likes me.

I catch Andie watching me and I think maybe this wasn't all about being perfect and sitting together and maybe there's a little bit of how are you doing are you going crazy today involved also. But then she smiles and brushes a piece of a leaf out of my hair with her hand and it isn't about her being a doctor and me being a patient at all.

"Thank you," I tell her. It's the first time I ever spoke to her. I mean without her doctoring me. Spoke to her like it was all my idea to speak.

"For what?" she asks.

I want to tell her the truth, I really do. But somehow, "For being someone who would brush a leaf out of my hair, for smiling to let me know it was all right, for inspiring me to live in this world, for being the love of my life," comes off as just a little too much. I think it would turn her doctor switch on, and instead I feel my face turn red as I try not to tell her I love her and that she smells good and I want to ask Violet how she tasted but I can't.

"Just because," I whisper, my head turned down, not willing to look at her, to be drawn into those soft brown eyes that own me.

I feel her watching me. I keep my head down, until the shouts of the boys playing ball draw her eyes away, and I look up, and watch her watching them, and it is wonderful again. Stepping into a warm towel just out of the dryer as you leave the shower, that's what she is. That's Andie.

"I'll play if you will," she says. She isn't looking at me, just staring straight ahead at Kareem and Pet Shop. I wonder whom she's asking, but Violet is obviously not paying any attention and I can't see her asking Stuart to play football. I think about running around on the grass with her, about throwing her the ball and her throwing it to me. Playing. Being a part of the game. I think about it too long.

"Let's go," Violet says, and I realize how stupid I was thinking I was the one being asked. Why would the ugly duckling ever go to the prom? Not when the swan that puts out is already spreading her wings for you. I recede, not wanting to watch, not wanting to see them having fun, playing, laughing, touching. Being together. Without me.

Violet looks at me, as if to say you had your chance, I gave you a five count, she was fair game after that. And she's right. I could have said yes, and maybe Andie would have pretended she was asking me and not Violet, and so it is my fault and I can't go to sleep to make it better.

"Burgers are done!" cries Sam, and we all go to a picnic table and put ketchup and pickles and tomatoes but no mustard I don't like mustard on them. Andie eats two burgers, I can't believe she can eat that much but I guess all that running around with Kareem and Pet Shop and Violet and not me why not me made her hungry. Kareem has three. I see Pet Shop drop a couple on the ground when no one else is looking. I keep an eye on them but they stay uneaten. Maybe the hedgehog is a vegetarian. I can't see the cow as a cannibal, and that monkey is probably still not climbing trees for him.

Violet grabs a hot dog. "Hey, Kareem," she says, and we all see her expertise displayed on the dog. Shy Boy starts rocking at the table, Andie scowls at her and Kareem gets a big smile. She pulls the hot dog out, half of it bitten off.

"Is that any way to treat a wiener?" Kareem asks.

Violet almost chokes on the hot dog as she laughs. Even Andie thought that one was funny, and she tries not to laugh at any of the sex jokes we make. But it is grill out day and the big tin foil episode appears to have faded without retribution and the sun is shining and the air is crisp and so we all laugh as we could if we were outside all the time. The real outside.

We eat and it is yummy. Fourth of July burgers, that is what they taste like, even if it is the second week of November.

"Happy Fourth of July!" I tell Stuart, and he gets all worried that the government has stolen seven months of his life. I explain about the taste of the burgers and he wants to go vomit them up in case the government has laced them with chemicals. Violet tells him to just breathe in the non-government fall air and be happy and he calms down.

I see Violet trying her foot massage under the picnic table with Kareem, but he just moves down the bench out of reach. Kareem is the best orderly we have, he is nice and only tranqs us when we really deserve it. I'm not sure why he doesn't like Violet. Everyone else does – even Andie, although she won't admit it. I remember how her face flushed when Violet kissed her. She never said she didn't like it. And she played football with her.

After we eat, we all lay back on the grass, watching the clouds push across the mostly clear sky. It was the best day of our lives, I think. Each day since Andie got here has been the best day. Even with Glen and Theodore gone; I know they are happy, that they are where they belong, so it is okay to have a best day.

"I see a pig," Andie says, lying next to me on the grass. Pet Shop looks around, checking for a lost member of his herd, I suppose. "No, Herbert," she explains, "that cloud up there. Doesn't it look like a pig?"

Large, solid body, on all fours, crouching. Big nose, heavy face, breathing in mine. The carpet isn't as soft as the bed. There will be marks again, I know. Evidence that Mom will never see. Never admit to seeing, anyway. The toast will be buttered twice in the morning, the eggs will burn, as everyone hides in the kitchen.

"Yes," I tell her, "it looks like a pig."

I wish I could see it like she does. I never had this before, this lying on the grass and looking at clouds and pretending they were wonderful wispy creations of all sorts of pure goodness and not evil nightmare monsters lurking in the dark, grabbing at you in the hallway, pushing you down.

"The one above it," I say, describing the one that looks like a pillow muffling my screams, "that's a nice fluffy pillow to put behind your back and read a book by, isn't it?"

"Sure it is," she agrees. "And look, that one could be a fuzzy caterpillar."

It doesn't look like a caterpillar to me. Not even close. But I don't tell her. I smile and pretend I can see into her world, pretend I am letting her see into mine. Because even pretending to share her vision makes this still the best day ever.

Sixteen: Shy Boy On The Couch

We have about an hour before lights out. This is pretty much the only time we watch television. There are only a couple channels, and most of them suck. They never put the news on, only safe things like Wheel of Fortune or Lawrence Welk or This Old House. Like they are ever going to let us use a power saw. It would be neat to knock a couple walls out and build an indoor bowling alley here. Although the odds of them letting us sling around sixteen pound bowling balls are pretty slim too.

Stuart refuses to watch any television at all – waves or radiation or something like that. Violet only likes Wheel of Fortune, she tries to guess dirty words until they reveal too many letters and they don't fit anymore. I don't really care what show is on — if I can't build a bowling alley why bother?

Shy Boy is sitting next to us on the couch. He smells okay today. Not like coffee like Andie smells but like mushrooms or cabbage or something that isn't exactly flowery but isn't spoiled either. Woodsy maybe? Anyway, he looks better without the earplug.

"Do you like him?" Violet asks. She caught me staring at Shy Boy. My face turns red. "It's okay if you do, I'm willing to share. I can even show you what he likes," she tells me, and I hide my face in my hands.

My hands are pulled away. I open my eyes to see it is Shy Boy, not Violet, who holds my hands. He is looking at me – actually looking at me – with what appears to be recognition and coherence and maybe, maybe a little touch of puppy dog be my first girlfriend can I carry your books love? Looking at me, not at Violet even if she is the one who traded for his radio and who rubbed his dick and called him sweetie, looking at me and not her? He is not Andie, he smells different and he is Shy Boy and I want to call him Gordon now. I want to but then he'll know I maybe like him.

He touches my face and I flinch and it is another man not him but I cannot help it and I flinch. He pulls back and I reach for his hand and put it back on my face and whisper, "It's okay, Shy Boy. It's okay."

Violet isn't angry or jealous. She guides my hand down to Shy Boy's lap but I tell her I can't do that I'm not ready and she is still not angry I love her she says it is okay she will help me be okay with everything again.

I squeeze Shy Boy's hand, and he squeezes back, and I know he knows what I know and it doesn't scare me. He isn't in my mind like Theodore was. It's a nice-that-he-knows knowledge and not an invading all-consuming threat. We resume watching Wheel of Fortune.

"BALL SUCKING WHORE," Violet tells Pat Sajak. There aren't any S's, but that is still her guess. Stuart giggles. I guess it's funny to hear Violet say that even if you aren't watching the show.

Kareem walks over, turns off the television. "Come on, Kareem," Violet says, "just one more puzzle. I am positive the next one has DICK in it."

"Sorry, people, it's lights out time. Off to bed."

Violet smiles, leaning into him, looking up at his six foot nine inch frame. "Want to come and play a little more touch football?"

He laughs, not taking her seriously. He never falls for it. "Not tonight, Violet, you'll have to play without me. Now go on, you have five minutes before lock down."

She pouts, but he is steadfast. Kareem is a really good guy. Or gay. We go to bed. I wave goodnight to Shy Boy and he waves back. At me, I think. Unless Violet was waving too.

Seventeen: All In The Family

When did he go from Daddy to Dad? I wonder. I am hiding from him again. I cannot remember the change. I know there was a time when he would play Barbie with me and hold me on his lap and not lift up my skirt and pull down my panties while I was sitting there. But I don't know when that was. Maybe if I could go back there, to that time when innocence still existed, and make it all right again, I could live with myself. With them. Maybe then it wouldn't be my fault. If I could have slept through that first time maybe he would have stopped and life would have turned out how it was supposed to. The way it did in all the fairy tales.

He is looking for me. I am holding my breath, hoping the closet will serve as a better hiding spot than the laundry room did last night. The door opens, he pushes the clothes aside and I am found. I yell "Base, I'm on Base" but it doesn't matter he isn't playing by the rules and it hurts.

He pulls me out of the closet and pushes me on the bed. At least it isn't the carpet, my back and butt won't have rug burns. I hear the belt buckle hit the floor and I start sobbing. He pauses, as if my cries have reminded him who he is and who I am and what isn't supposed to be happening and how he is supposed to protect me from this and that I am a little girl and he is a daddy but he isn't Daddy anymore he is Dad and I can't remember when that changed. And he can't remember either and he resumes and I am screaming and he puts the pillow over my mouth because last time he used his hand and I bit him.

I hear the door open and she is there and then it slams shut and he is off of me and running after her. I pray that this means it is over that she will save me, that now she can't deny what is happening and she will make him undo everything and we will be a family and not have to pretend anymore.

I wake up and it is breakfast time and I cry into my pillow. Because at least in the dream I could hope that it would be okay in the morning that she would fix it all but it is now instead and I remember back to that morning when he read even more of the paper and she made waffles with extra strawberries and cream and didn't say a god damn word about it ever.

I am late for breakfast. It doesn't really matter if the eggs are cold or the bacon is sitting in the grease because I haven't been able to eat either since, well since ever. Since the apple was eaten and paradise was lost and the inferno burned. I grab a jelly doughnut. Even on bad days jelly tastes good.

Shy Boy smiles at me but I can't handle him today, I can't handle the possibility that if I was normal, if the world didn't have this great big building ready to drop on me, that I could be with someone, even a weirdo like Shy Boy.

"Good morning, Vietnam," the hedgehog greets me with when I sit down at the breakfast table. I ignore the invisible animal and his crazy keeper. Not that Pet Shop was even talking to me.

"There's a moooooon out tonight," the cow tries, but I am not up for puns or satire or parodies or whatever it is when a cow moos out a song.

"Full moon has one more day, Daphne, and then we are safe again," Stuart tells me.

As if we are ever safe. How can we be safe when in the middle of the night after the best day ever he can come and get me across space and time and memory and make me the dirty girl whose fault it is all over again? Even after Andie the goddess lay beside me and watched clouds and Shy Boy squeezed my hand and we had Fourth of July hamburgers. If he can do that, then how will there ever be enough good in the mix of humanity which I am no longer so certain Theodore was right about me being part of to counteract that kind of poison?

I think of Glen and the lightning bolt and Theodore and his sea of aliens turned human and I am embarrassed that I count their efforts so miserly. That I throw away so easily what cost them so greatly to give me. I put my jelly doughnut down, turn to Shy Boy, and give him my very best good morning. I ask the hedgehog how his day is going. I thank the cow for giving us milk. Only after all of that do I turn to Violet.

"I missed you last night," I tell her.

"I'm sorry, baby," she says. "I thought you needed a night alone, after all that hand holding with Shy Boy."

"I'm never alone at night. You know that."

She looks so sad. "I know, Daphne. That will change, I promise. We're going to make that all go away someday. Andie will help us do that for you, you'll see. She'll help us all. Before you know it, we'll be one big happy family."

"We are family," the hedgehog says.

"Well, except for maybe Pet Shop," Violet adds.

Eighteen: The Bad Doctor Returns

Doctor Martin sure knows how to ruin a party. We just get settled in for group, Andie was letting Shy Boy stay since Violet was keeping her hands off of him, Stuart wasn't panicking since I told him we would go and recalibrate his triangle reflection things after lunch and Pet Shop had his herd under control, when Genghis Khan makes his return. He stands there, smiling, pretending he is a doctor and not a son of a bitch, holding his clipboard as if to forestall any charge by Violet to his privates. Andie doesn't even pretend to be happy to see him.

"Good morning, Doctor MacPherson," he says, as if he didn't remember she asked him to call her Andie. As if he wasn't carrying a swarm of locusts with him.

"Doctor Martin," she returns in as icy a voice as a warm zephyr can carry. "To what do we owe the honor of your presence today?"

He stumbles a little at the reception but blusters through anyway. Warning shots fired and ignored, open season in my opinion. I try to get Violet's attention, try to persuade her to go for his balls but she ignores me. What a fine time to become a prude.

"I just thought I would observe today, no special reason. See if everything is going acceptably. Under control. Since the treatment," he adds, smiling at Violet.

I cannot believe she isn't crotch diving after that, but maybe Andie's calm demeanor is having a positive influence on her. Andie is tapping her pencil on her notepad, acting like there is nothing in the world she would like better than for Doctor Martin to observe. As if it was her idea, and not his, and about damn time he showed up. Times like this she looks more hot than cute. I think about Violet tasting her, about how it would feel to feel her lips pressed against mine. I can't help it.

"Everything is going fine," Andie says. "While I don't feel the treatment was necessary, it doesn't appear to have harmed my efforts. No, I think we are all making progress despite your treatment."

"Doctor MacPherson, I will not have my treatments questioned, certainly not in front of the patients. I am the head of staff here, in case you have forgotten."

"Of course you are, Doctor Martin, I'm sorry. I didn't mean to... question your methods. I merely wanted you to know they are all doing fine."

"Hmmph. Very well. Why don't you continue with the session? As I said, I am just here to observe."

So we sit and twiddle our thumbs for a couple minutes. Eventually the hedgehog breaks out in a chorus of "I am a Rock," Stuart giggles and we begin talking.

Violet starts it, as usual. "Daphne and Shy Boy, sitting in a tree..."

Andie looks at me, then at Shy Boy. "Violet, let's not tease anyone, okay? Daphne, do you want to talk about anything – anything about Gordon, maybe?"

I am the shy one now. I hang my head, ears turning red, face flushed. I don't want her to know that I like Shy Boy. Then maybe she won't think that I like her. I've never had a boyfriend. *He* doesn't count.

"No," I whisper.

Shy Boy leans over, takes my hand. I pull it away.

"Gordon, it looks like Daphne doesn't want anyone to touch her right now, so please don't try that again."

He looks like I cut his hand off, like there was an opening and I came running up and slammed the door in his face. Like I felt when... I change my mind and reach for his hand, give it a little squeeze and let it go. His balloon is in the sky again and I don't have to cry.

"That was very nice, Daphne. It was very nice to show Gordon you weren't mad at him. Still, Gordon, please ask Daphne next time, okay?"

"Moooooning over you," says the cow, and I flush red again.

Doctor Martin is scribbling a lot on his notepad. Daphne hardly ever writes on hers. I think it is there to keep her hands from wandering up and pushing those black-rimmed glasses up that perky nose. She shouldn't bother; it looks cute when she does it.

"You can only observe you can't act I stopped you and you can't read my mind," Stuart states to Doctor Martin.

He raises his gaze from his notepad. He doesn't answer Stuart, just looks over at Andie, mouths "Just observing," to her and returns to his notepad.

"Stuart," Andie says, "I promise you that none of us can read your mind. Remember, you are a human being. You have a name, you are unique."

"But part of humanity, Andie, aren't we all part of humanity?" I beseech her – if this has changed then I will not be happy.

"Absolutely, Daphne, we are all part of humanity. That's why we respect each other, why we must confer dignity and privacy and love."

"I know you can't read our minds, Andie. I believe that you are human. He, however," Stuart gestures toward Doctor Martin, "is an entirely different matter. His mind reading capabilities have not been determined."

"Spies like us," informs the hedgehog.

Stuart puts his arms across his chest, gives a nod of affirmation. Once the hedgehog speaks, Stuart pretty much takes it as gospel.

"I will personally vouch for Doctor Martin, Stuart. He is most certainly human. I mean, look at him, surely the government could build a better robot than that!"

Violet adds, "And I know at least part of him is flesh. And boner."

Stuart giggles, I laugh, the hedgehog goes wild. Even Shy Boy smiles at that one. I think he is listening to us more now, since the earplug isn't constantly filling his head with sports scores.   Doctor Martin just keeps scribbling furiously in his notepad.

Andie settles back in her chair, stifling her own laughter. After we all calm down, she smoothes her skirt that shows just a little bit of leg, my but what a pretty figure she makes in her skirt that could twirl around her if we were dancing, and I bet she square dances and sits on bales of hay, sipping apple cider between songs.

"Herbert," she asks, and we look around before we remember that that is Pet Shop's name, "how are you doing today?"

"Doing all right, future's so bright, gotta wear shades," replies the hedgehog.

"I am glad your furry friend is doing fine, but how are you, Herbert?" she asks again.

"He'd be better if ya dinna keep harassin' the poor boy, lady." I'm not sure who is speaking; it's hard to tell when they are all invisible. I think it is the same one who harassed the hedgehog the first day Pet Shop ate with us. But God only knows what particular invisible animal it is.

"I'm not harassing you, Herbert, I just want to talk to you occasionally. It's fine to hear from your animals, but couldn't we have a word from you now and then?"

Pet Shop – Herbert – looks at her, glances around as if seeing if any of his herd is willing to take his place again, but I guess they are off grazing. "Okay, Andie. I'm okay. That's all," he says, then unties and ties and unties et cetera his shoes.

"Thank you, Herbert. That wasn't so hard, now was it? Okay, I think we are done for now, I will see you again this afternoon."

I'm not sure Doctor Martin agreed with Andie's assessment of our progress but at least he escaped without Violet latching onto his crotch. Maybe that part was a disappointment; he was probably looking for an excuse to shock her again.

Nineteen: Recalibrating The Reflection Things

Stuart is ecstatic at the effectiveness of his anti government meta ray wave insaturation deflection device. He swears his mind has been untouched since we installed it. I think his mind has been touched in all kinds of ways.

"No, not that way. Angle it toward me," he tells Pet Shop, who is once again up a tree without his monkey. Pet Shop moves the triangle reflection thing until Stuart is happy with the angle and crawls along the branch to the next one.

I look around for the screech owl but don't see him. Too bad, I think Pet Shop would like a visit from his feathered compatriot. The wind starts to pick up a little and one of the triangles falls out of the tree.

"Mayday! Mayday!" Stuart shouts. "Everybody keep thinking peas and carrots until I replace the reflection triangle!" He runs over and picks up the triangle. There is a tear in it where it had pulled off of the branch. He folds it over, reshaping it, then goes back to the tree and hands it up to Pet Shop. Pet Shop replaces it and the device is operational again. Stuart tells us we can stop thinking about peas and carrots.

We walk around the gravestones, fixing the foil antennae where they have fallen. There are twenty-seven stones, each with a different number, each with a different date. All the stones are the same shape and size, there is nothing to distinguish number three seven dash four three three from number three seven dash eight three five except about five feet of longitude. Or maybe latitude, I never remember which is which.

Violet leans down and kisses number three seven dash four three three, and I realize there is still a difference. That these people – people, not numbers – are just as much a part of our commonality as Glen and Theodore, that no matter what THEY do they cannot take that away from them. Or us.

I join Shy Boy by the base of the big tree with the triangle reflection devices. He is staring at his radio, nestled in the crook where a large branch juts off of the main trunk. I know he misses it. I want to thank him for letting Stuart use it. I want to love him. I settle for reaching out and giving his hand a squeeze.

He pulls it away. Shy Boy pulls his hand away from me! I stand there, mouth agape, completely shocked that he would do that! Then, even more from left field than his pulling his hand away, he grins. And reaches for my hand! I am so startled by this that I let him take my hand and hold it. Shy Boy actually teased me.

Violet must have seen this because next thing I know she is whispering in my ear, "He must really like you, if he is teasing you. Little boys only tease little girls they like. Little boys pull on little girls' pigtails. Little boys have pigtails too, just in front instead of behind. Don't you want to show him how much you like him? Come on, Daphne, you know he wants you to." She takes my hand, the one Shy Boy isn't holding, and moves it down in front of him. I pull it back.

"No, Violet, I can't do that," I tell her, trying not to cry because I am happy I am holding his hand but I am scared and don't want to think about what Shy Boy wants me to do just like what *he* wanted me to do all those nights and I won't.

I open my eyes and I am still holding Shy Boy's hand and he maybe looks a little disappointed but he still looks happy too and I think maybe it will be okay.

Stuart announces that everything is in perfect working order, that we are once more safe from government mind control, at least until tomorrow, so we walk back. Pet Shop keeps looking over his shoulder, but we don't see the owl.

Twenty: Andie Tells Us A Story

We get to afternoon group and are glad to see that Doctor Martin isn't there. Probably off observing some of the other crazies. Or recovering from hand cramps due to all his frantic scribbling during our morning session.

Andie is very quiet. She looks at her notepad, not at us. We sit, silently, not sure what is going on. Not even the hedgehog is willing to start us out.

Finally she stands up, smoothing her skirt – yes, the nice twirling barn dance, rolling in the hay, wonder what color her panties – stop, stop, stop she is nice she is not like that.

"I had a good conversation with Doctor Martin," she begins. Oh God, the bastard got to her! How can any conversation with him be good?

She continues, "He agreed that our group is having positive effects. That we are making progress." She smiles. I am still waiting for the catch. There is no way he doesn't have some nefarious scheme, some dastardly plot behind his seeming good will.

"And he has also agreed that his personal observations are not necessary." Sweet Jesus, did I hear that correctly? No more evil emperor? No more mister nasty?

I can't help it. I hug her. I even get there before Violet, who was just looking at a hug as a way to feel her breasts pressed against her own. Sam, bless that mean old orderly, has at least learned enough to see when it is a hug and not an attack, and doesn't even take a step toward us.

I think Andie is as surprised as Violet that I got there first. Her eyes even mist a little – over me! Shy Boy looks a little jealous. After the hug I squeeze his hand to let him know he is still my sweetie.

"Great Caesar's Ghoooost!" cries the cow.

Stuart sat there. He was the only one who didn't act happy about Doctor Martin's absence. Violet notices it first, I am still reliving the hug and Andie's soft brown eyes getting misty and how she felt in her skirt and her sweater against me not like Violet but nice not needy but sharing and warm and nice.

Violet asks him, "What's up, Stuart?"

"A direction away from the center of gravity of a celestial body. But that's not important." He points at the camera in the upper corner of the room, the red light blinking, I'm watching, I'm watching, I'm watching. "That is."

Andie sees what he is pointing at and sighs. "Stuart, the camera is not important. It is not hurting you; it is not reading your mind."

"Then what is it doing?" he asks.

"Stuart, we have to have it on. It is recording us — I won't deny that — but only for my personal use. It helps me to understand everything we talk about. I promise that's all. Nobody else sees the tape – not Doctor Martin, not the government – nobody. I'm the only one who has access to it."

Stuart turns to Pet Shop. "What's the hedgehog say?"

"He isn't here," Pet Shop says. "I can't find him anywhere. Nobody but the cow has talked to me all day, and frankly, he isn't much of a conversationalist."

That is the most I have ever heard Pet Shop say.

"Good Lord!" Stuart exclaims, "It is worse than I thought. Without the hedgehog, we are doomed. Doomed, I say!"

Andie settles him down. He was about to stand up and start on another rant, which only would have led to Sam tranqing him. She takes his hand, caresses his forearm with those gentle fingers that could erase all memory of pain and sorrow and emptiness with one soft lingering brush against your skin, and he takes a deep breath and sits back in his chair.

"I am sure the hedgehog will be back when he is needed. Now do you trust me, Stuart? Have I ever lied to you?"

"But the hedgehog –"

"Isn't who I am asking, Stuart," she interrupts. "I am asking you – do you trust me?"

And he does. I can tell. How could you not trust the soul of humanity, the heart of the sun? How could there be any doubt when an angel from heaven takes you in her arms and breaths manna into your face and you drink it in and you drink her in and you wonder how she tasted and Violet tells you sweet, sweet as fresh strawberries that you picked in a meadow that *he* was never ever in.

Stuart admits it. He has to. "Yes," he says, "I trust you, Andie. But I still want to talk to the hedgehog."

"So do I," she says. "Herbert, please tell us if the hedgehog comes back. And if you get tired of talking to the cow, please come see me. I may not hold a candle to the conversational skills of the hedgehog but I am pretty sure I can outtalk the cow."

"Okay, Andie," Pet Shop replies. "I'm okay for now, but maybe later."

"How do we know?" Violet asks. "How do we really know we can trust you?" Who is she kidding? I think this is just a ploy because she doesn't like not being the center of attention, not being the one that everyone wants to… touch.

Andie looks at her, looks at her not me, and I am jealous and it burns and I squeeze Shy Boy's hand so tight that he lets out a little yelp.

Andie lets this pass, she just keeps looking at Violet, that "I am the light, the lord, the essence of all that matters" smile illuminating the room and Violet just stares back and obviously has shields on full force, look out Captain I don't think she can take anymore.

"How can we believe we could ever be like you?" Violet asks. The real question. Not about trust or faith or who wants to help us but how could we ever, ever be anything close to the wondrous being before us?

"I'm not special," she says to us, "I am just like you. I have my problems, I have my emotions, and I get scared too."

"Don't say if you cut me do I not bleed because that's a road we aren't supposed to go down," Stuart says.

"No, no cutting or bleeding. Not on the outside." She looks straight at me. "But inside, I have my demons and fears and nights when I wake up screaming."

"You do?" I wonder at the possibility, that *he* could ever penetrate her dreams. That she was ever forced to... to be me. "You have nightmares, like I do?"

She takes my hands, looks me in the eyes. I cannot see any demons in her irises. I am certain I am unable to hide the ones swimming in my own. "Daphne, I know you have very frightening dreams. I know what has happened in the past haunts you. I won't pretend that my own nightmares are anything like yours, but I do have them. There are... incidents in my past that visit me when I sleep, that leave me trembling and sweating and crying. But they do not own me. They do not keep me from living in the present. That is what I am offering to you. I cannot make them go away, only you can do that. I cannot make the past any brighter, and better, any safer than it really was. What I can do, what we can do together, is learn how to accept what happened, and how to keep it in the past where it belongs. It doesn't have to be our master; it doesn't have to keep us from enjoying today."

Her impassioned plea, her vulnerability, her empathy, wash over me, overwhelm me, drown me. I know she is telling me the truth, about wanting to help, about her own nightmares, but especially about how she doesn't know just how bad mine are. It is obvious that *he* isn't a part of her nights; that she had been able to sleep through until morning and *he* never woke her and she never heard the belt buckle hit the floor or wet her pants because she smelled his cigar in the hallway.

"Tell me about the dreams, Daphne," she pleads and I don't want to because either she won't understand or worse she will and then he would have tainted her too and she wouldn't be pure and she would have part of him in her and I could never love her without loving him too and he would win.

She purses her lips. God! How does someone do that? A simple tightening of a couple facial muscles and I am pulled to her, she is opening me and I am fighting it trying not to contaminate her, trying to keep her safe so there is still Base so I can still call Base and not be tagged.

Her voice is gentle, soft, intoxicating. "Daphne, let me tell you a story. I was twenty-two, just out of college, on an internship. I was dating exactly who my mother wanted me to date, a twenty-five year old doctor in his second year of residency with a big bright smile and blue eyes that would have made Robert Redford jealous."

She takes a deep breath and continues. "He was tan and bronze and had just enough chest hair to let you know he was a man but not a hairy ape. Not so much that when you ran your hands over it the hairs caught or tugged or made him wince. He was perfect."

She isn't looking at me so much as through me now. I hang on every word of this fairy tale, this prince that I had never found but she had, and I am waiting for happily ever after but I can tell from the clouds in her eyes that there is a storm on the horizon.

"Within six months we were engaged. Mother and Father couldn't have been prouder. Their little tom boy had turned into a woman and was going to have the white picket fence and a doctor, 'My goodness,' my mother said, 'well I suppose you can stop this silly internship now'."

Even Sam is all ears, leaning close, straining to catch every word Andie says.

"And so I dropped out of the program. I went to bridal shops and read bridal magazines and picked out blue and silver napkins for the reception. My parents were wonderful and loving and it was all because I was playing the part for them. For him. For the American Dream. And I was hating every second of it but it was too late we were engaged and the hall was reserved and he was perfect and Mother loved him and Father smoked cigars with him on the veranda."

She sits there, remembering the events, and no one moved. No one talked, no one breathed. No one wanted to break this spell, to give her any reason to stop.

"So we got married. Mother said it was just the champagne when I told her how he pushed me on our wedding night when I told him he was drunk, that he didn't mean anything by it."

"Father told me to work things out three months later when I showed up on his doorstep with a broken nose. He said marriages take work, take effort. Mother pretended not to see the bruises under my makeup when we met for lunch."

I taste the salt of my tears as they roll down my cheek and over my lips. My heart is breaking, my soul crying out in empathy, in ecstasy for the shared pain, for the common bond I feel with Andie.

"The third time in the emergency room was the last. The doctor recognized me from my internship and took me to a safe house. I was divorced a year later. It was another two years before I got the courage to see my parents. We're on speaking terms now, but they never did understand why I left. Why we couldn't work it out. Why I couldn't handle getting beaten by my husband every time he tied one on."

"I'm so sorry, Andie," I tell her. "I'm so sorry," I repeat, hugging her, crying onto her shoulder, and feeling her own tears as she holds me against her.

"It's okay, Daphne. Telling the story helps. I get a little more of me back from him every time I tell it. I tell it so I know it is part of the past and not what is happening to me now. Can you understand that?"

I just cry on her shoulder. I understand it, but that doesn't mean I can do it. She lets me cry, even when the bell rings and our time is up, she remains, holding me.

Twenty-One: More Wheel Of Fortune

"HUMPING HIPPOS," Violet guesses. Pet Shop smiles at the hippopotamus reference. Violet's in a good mood, bouncing up and down on the couch every time a letter is turned over that doesn't mess up her answer.

"Did anyone know that about Andie?" I ask. "Did anyone think she could ever have been one of us?"

"Once you accept that she isn't one of them," Stuart says, "how could she help but be one of us?"

"Suffragette City," says the cow. It's really something the hedgehog would have said. I think the cow must miss the little bugger too.

Shy Boy reaches over and pats my hand. I smile and he smiles back. Someday maybe I will do it with him. He doesn't seem like he looms in dark passages ready to jump and make me bleed and howl from pain and scrape my nails into the floor until they break. He doesn't seem that way at all.

Violet claps when the S is turned over at the end of the second word. "HUMPING HIPPOS!" she says, "It could still be HUMPING HIPPOS!"

Violet is ignoring the question. I think she wants Andie to remain apart. I think she is afraid of Andie. Afraid of her sweet taste. Afraid of her sweater and skirt and pursed lips and curling hair over her ears. I don't think she likes it that Andie has dreams like I do.

"Maybe you could visit her, Violet. Help her sleep like you do for me." It's not that I don't want Violet with me, it's just that Andie deserves her more than I do. Andie's worth saving. Andie needs to be whole.

"H, you stupid slut," she tells the contestant. "Give me a friggin' H!"

After they turn over a T instead and her hippos have no chance to be humping anymore, she turns to me. "No," she says. "Andie doesn't need me. You do."

"But –"

"I said no! Weren't you even listening to her? No, you were too busy crying on her shoulder and sniffing her hair and pushing against her boobs, weren't you? She doesn't need fixing, she fixed herself. Hell, she wasn't even raped."

I curl into a ball in a corner of the sofa, dragging a blanket over me. Shy Boy tries to pull the blanket off to check on me but I kick at his hands until he leaves me alone. Violet doesn't check to see if I am okay but I don't care she doesn't understand she was never forced she is always the one making other people do stuff with her. I stay there until Kareem says lights out and I go to bed and hide my head under the pillow and wait for Violet to come and hold me and she doesn't. I pull my sleeve up and try to smell Andie's tears on it but I can't tell if they are hers or mine.

Twenty-Two: In Which We Are No Longer Safe

After breakfast we go out to check on the cemetery. Violet isn't speaking to me. Whenever I try to talk to her she says "Save it for Andie." Fine, if that's the way she wants to be I will.

"Red rum! Red rum!" the cow cries when we get to the broken down fence.

Stuart's hands fly to his head; complete disaster has struck. All the triangle reflection devices, all the tin foil antennae, all the miscellaneous pieces of his anti government mind reading device thing are in tatters. Shy Boy runs to the base of the big oak and starts crying. The shattered remains of his radio lay on the ground.

"No!" Stuart cries, running around the gravestones until he finally trips and lands on the unmown grass. He beats his fists into the ground, screaming his frustration until he wears down from his efforts.

Violet and I call a truce as we try to console him. "There, there," I say, "it will be okay. This is the last night of the full moon anyway; we will just be careful, okay?"

"I'll keep you busy, if you want," Violet tells him. "They can't read your mind if you're in the middle of an orgasm, that's a proven fact."

"How did they know?" he asks, his eyes wild. "Who ratted me out?"

He grabs Pet Shop by the shirt. "Did the hedgehog crack? What did they offer him, Eastern Europe?"

"He wouldn't," Pet Shop insists, "he's the best one I have. He would never tell."

Stuart lets him go. "No, you're right, what was I thinking. He's no stool pigeon." He turns back to Pet Shop. "You don't have any of those, do you?"

"No," he says. "Right now just a cow, a missing hedgehog and that damn monkey. But he's never around, he doesn't even know about the cemetery."

"Maybe it was the wind," I offer. "It was picking up when we recalibrated yesterday."

"So you are saying that maybe the President didn't order the head of the CIA to send an operative on a covert mission to destroy the one device in the western hemisphere capable of withstanding their mental assault? That he wouldn't try to disable the only hope we have of autonomy, of individual thought, of self-command? Don't be absurd."

He paces back and forth among the unnamed dead. "However," he adds, "the covert mission could have been the propagation of weather control in this specific locale so as to make it seem that it was a natural event that brought about this catastrophe." Stuart pauses then snaps his fingers. "There is only one way we can ensure our safety tonight."

"What's that?" I ask, dreading the answer, bracing myself for some foolhardy scheme that would doubtlessly end up with one of us tranquilized.

"Andie. The lady must be informed."

And so it was that Stuart decided that Andie could, in fact, be trusted.

Twenty-Three: The Lady Is Informed

Andie must have known something was up the minute she sat down for afternoon group. Stuart was all jittery and Pet Shop was petting the cow and Shy Boy was rocking back and forth. Sam was only a step away from us, he could see we were all jumpy and I don't think he wanted to be caught off guard.

"Well, it looks like something is going on that I don't know about it. Did somebody get a little too much sugar at lunch?" She doesn't seem like Andie when she is not quite sure what is going on. But she is still really, really cute when she is curious about it. Like a cat who wants to know what you are reading and absolutely has to sit on your lap and stick his nose in your book. Just in case this one time the book ends up being a can of tuna.

Stuart's hand shoots up, almost at attention or in salute.

"My lady Andie, I bear most distressing news."

"What is it, Stuart?" she asks, returning the solemnity in his tone with her own angelic voice, speaking to him as a princess would to her messenger, a queen to her advisor. Connecting with him as no other therapist ever has been willing to.

"THEY have compromised the anti government meta ray wave insaturation deflection device. It lies in ruins, and we are defenseless. I fear Camelot is lost."

"Are you sure it is broken? Can you fix it?" she asks, even though I know that she knows there is no such device, not one that would work, nor would there need to be, since THEY don't exist.

"Alas, it is beyond my skill to repair. But maybe..."

"Yes?" she asks.

"Maybe if you looked at it you could heal it."

"I'm not sure what you are asking, but if you want me to look at it I will."

"Please," Stuart asks, "would you?"

So we all go off to the cemetery and she sees the mess of tin foil and broken radio parts. And she sees the gravestone with number three seven dash four three three and a single date and the twenty-six other unnamed gravestones surrounded by the broken down fence amid the unmown grass. She kneels beside the gravestone that Violet always kisses and she looks up at Stuart and her comprehension of all that he has told her is so palpable that I want to cry with joy.

And Stuart sees that she believes everything that he has ever said and that she understands and that she will make it all better and he falls into her arms by the gravestone that Violet always kisses.

Shy Boy picks up the pieces of his radio and Pet Shop screeches in case his owl friend – the visible one — is around and I laugh at how happy Stuart is and how safe and protected he is in her arms.

We walk around the gravestones and Andie looks at each and every one of them. She copies all of the numbers and all of the dates down on her notepad. She shows us how all the dates are over thirty years ago, some over fifty, and tells us not to be scared, that we will never end up here, that she will always know who we are.

"There's a mooooon out tonight," the cow cries, but Stuart ignores him. He knows Andie will keep out the mind readers. This is the best day ever, and so it is worth at least one night of protection from government mind reading radio waves.

Twenty-Four: Dreams Of A Happy Nature

I am in my pajamas and there is the smell of Christmas in the air. Gingerbread men and crackling logs in the fireplace and hot cocoa and Uncle Bob's pipe. I smile at Daddy and he tells me I am his favorite little girl in the whole wide world. I run across the living room, the carpet feels nice on my bare feet, and jump on the sofa. I curl up with my blanket and my doll and listen to Mommy hum Christmas carols as she puts up all the decorations.

Mommy is so pretty in her Santa overalls with the fluffy reindeer slippers and the jingle bells on her pockets. She taps me on the nose as she walks by and I giggle and we are so happy together.

We are curled up, all together under the blanket, watching the fire pop and crackle. It is so warm and toasty that no one wants to get up and I ask Mommy and Daddy to promise that we can live under the blanket in front of the fireplace forever and ever. And just before they promise Daddy's eyes get wide and says wait a minute what about Santa? And I decide that maybe we better not live under there forever or Santa might not find us and we won't get any presents. I hug Daddy and kiss him and thank him for saving Christmas. Mommy laughs and asks if she can have hugs and kisses even if she didn't save Christmas and I say of course Mommy and give them to her. But I don't hug her quite as hard or kiss her quite as many times as Daddy because he was the one who saved Christmas after all.

So we get out from under the blanket and go to my bedroom. Mommy watches me say my prayers and I remember everybody even Uncle Bob and then I crawl under the sheets and ask Mommy if it is okay if Daddy tucks me in tonight. She tussles my hair and says of course, the man who saved Christmas is responsible for all tucking-ins and when Daddy comes in and kisses me good night and tucks me in everything is perfect. I fall asleep and dream about all the presents we are going to get and how Daddy and Mommy and I will take them under the blanket in front of the fireplace and live together forever.

Twenty-Five: Discovering The Past, But Not Ours

When we get to the morning session Andie has a big surprise for us. We are going on a trip to the library! Stuart, Violet, Shy Boy, Pet Shop, Kareem – thank God, he is so much nicer than Sam – Andie and I all get in a van. Andie drives. I didn't know she could drive; I never had a chance to learn how to drive. I guess it makes sense, she has to get to work somehow. Sometimes I forget she doesn't live in the dorm with us. That she has a life in the outside world. Separate from us.

Andie is being mysterious and isn't telling us what the trip is about or why we are going. We ask Kareem but he just smiles and puts up his hands like he isn't in on it and it is all a surprise for him too. I like that he is as much in the dark as we are. That way it is something special not bad and it isn't just secret because we can't handle it.

"Is it a government library?" Stuart asks. "I won't go to a government library. They scan your retina and imprint secret codes on your memory nodes so when they capture you later they can see where you have been. They see everything you ever looked at. Everything."

"It's not a government library," Andie assures him. "It's at the college – a private college," she adds, stalling the protest that Stuart would have made over a state-funded school.

She lets us pick the radio station and soon we are all singing along with The Police. You haven't heard "Roxanne" until you've heard it inside a van from the funny farm. I bet she will change the station faster than you can say spit if they play "I'll Be Watching You" next.

We are on a country road, going past cornfields and dirt roads leading to farm houses and pastures with cows in them. Visible cows that don't as much as moo at us let alone quote song titles or badger the hedgehog. It's been I don't know how long since I saw the outside. I mean more than just the woods behind the dorm, the real outside where the fences aren't designed to keep people in as much as to say if you cross me then you are visiting the nice family who lives here. A perimeter of belonging instead of exclusion.

I wave at every single farmer, every car that passes us (Andie isn't what you would call a recklessly fast driver), every cow that doesn't moo. Shy Boy feels nice, sitting next to me on the seat. We are a little short on room in the middle seat but I don't mind as it is a pushing against a friend feeling, not a trapped so tight you will suffocate one.

It is a short drive, so Andie is able to avoid telling us anything about our secret mission – that was what she had to tell Stuart we were on to keep him from pestering her – before we pull into the parking lot at the library. Kareem is working overtime to keep us all together. Andie gives him a rope and everyone holds onto it and that works better.

We follow Andie into the library. Stuart giggles because we are all "shushing" each other, thinking no one has ever done that before in a library or thought it was funny. A couple of the people look at us but we stare at them until they turn away. Hah, if we couldn't handle a few looks or stare downs we would have poked our eyes out by now. These library people are folding like a couple pairs going up against a flush. I heard that in a movie once.

Andie takes us into a room that is set apart from the shelves of books and the people sitting in lounge chairs and on sofas drinking coffee and typing on lap top computers and surfing the Internet. Libraries aren't just books anymore. She closes the door and we gather around a big table that has lots of books and newspapers on it and everybody sits down and I am last and Stuart giggles and says the music stopped and I don't get to win the cake.

"I know you are all wondering why we are here today," she starts. We smile and nod and even Shy Boy pays attention to what she is saying. "Well, I did a lot of thinking after our session yesterday. A lot. About the cemetery, about what we talked about. About how you guys were right –"

Pet Shop raises his hand.

Andie pauses, looks at him inquiringly.

"We're not all guys," he says.

"Yes, you're right, it was just an expression. Sorry."

"Dude looks like a lady," opines the cow.

"Okay, well, anyway," Andie continues, "I was thinking about how you – all of you, guys and girls – were concerned about the people who had been buried there. And I completely agree with you, it wasn't right for them to be marked only by a number and a date. They deserve more – we all do, we all deserve to be recognized and respected. And that is why we are here, to correct a wrong, to honor them properly."

Stuart shakes his head animatedly, "No, it's no good, it won't work."

"But Stuart, I haven't even told you –"

"I'm not an idiot," he shouts, and Kareem moves next to him, trying to keep him in his seat. "It's obvious your plan is to disinter the bodies and rebury them under the bookshelves. But the government tracks all books; they will spot you as soon as the first page is opened."

"Stuart, that is not my plan."

"It isn't?" he asks. "Oh, well then, never mind."

"So what are we doing?" Violet asks. "We going to check out some books and read them dirty stories?"

Andie sighs. "No, if you would let me –"

Kareem breaks in. "How about ghost stories? Are we going to read them ghost stories?" He starts laughing. I think he knew Andie didn't want to get interrupted again. Not by us, anyway, but Kareem doing it made it even more like we were all here together. Not doctor and orderly and patients but just people.

Andie gives him a dirty look, but she can't hold it very long and soon she is laughing too and Stuart giggles and Pet Shop is pounding the table and I laugh with them too. I see one of the library people give us a look through the window to the room but we just keep laughing. They let crazy people get away with anything that doesn't involve pointy objects.

After we settle down, Andie once more starts to explain the whole thing to us. We do our best to keep it down to a couple snickers so we can hear her. We do want to know, it's just so much fun being out that we want everything to last twice as long as normal, to stretch it out like walking home after you saw the best movie ever and you want to trap that feeling of happily ever after and you know as soon as the door closes you have to go back to reality so you take the long way home and hope you never get there.

"Okay, we are here," she says, pretending to be all serious and not looking at Kareem because he will just make her laugh again, "to make things better. For the people in the cemetery. And in a way for us too, and for anyone who might visit the cemetery in the future. What I want to do – what I want us to do – is give them back their names."

We aren't laughing or snickering or even trying not to laugh or snicker. Or anything close to that. We are sitting in silence as her words sink deeper and deeper into our souls. Give them back their names, I think, and I see a world where no one is against me and everyone matters and I am a person and part of humanity but still special, still unique, give them back their names.

Stuart looks at his savior, shaking with the enormity of what she is giving them – giving us. "My lady," he whispers, "you would de-fang the dragon itself."

"De-fang, hell," Violet says, "you're going to cut off his balls."

Violet's words move us from the reverent awe we felt to sheer joy at the action Andie was proposing. I squeeze Shy Boy's hand, and even if he doesn't quite understand what is going on he can sense my happiness and he grins back at me. Pet Shop high fives Kareem, and Andie is smiling at our response to her idea. I never want to leave this room. We can sit here and talk about how wonderful Andie is and what she will lead us to and wave at the library people through the window and feel this utter and complete happiness forever.

Andie picks up one of the books from the table. "This is how we will start. We have several books and newspapers from the library archives here. I am hoping that we can read through these and find out the names of some of the people who were being cared for. Once we find that out, we are going to make a plaque with all of the names that we can find. That way, anyone who visits the cemetery will know the names of the people who lived back then, and who might be buried there."

"How do we know what name belongs to what number?" I ask. "How can we tell we have it right?"

"Well, Daphne, we won't be a hundred percent sure. Those records aren't around anymore. But it isn't important if we have the exact name and number matching, the idea is that we are going to honor every person we can find who lived here. Their names, their spirits, are what matters. Not whether they are buried under this particular rock or a different one."

I accept the truth in her words. I think of Glen and Theodore and the unification of the cosmos and decide a hunk of decayed flesh and old bones really isn't the point of it all. I think if she is willing to care about a bunch of numbered crazies from fifty years ago then maybe she will remember my name too. Maybe some warm summer evening when a breeze brings a hint of a coming thunderstorm she will reflect on how Daphne was real. I smile, thinking of Andie thinking of me.

I pick up a newspaper and start looking.

Twenty-Six: The Hitchhiker

Other than an incident with Violet and the photocopy machine, we get out of the library without creating too much chaos. And she was right, why would they have a copy machine if you weren't supposed to see what your butt looked like? Andie was upset with her, but Kareem laughed. I saw Shy Boy put the photocopy in his pocket. I guess I can't blame him. She does have a cute butt.

So Kareem has us grab onto the rope and he and Andie lead us back to the van. We did pretty good, we found stories about at least a dozen patients, we have some names to go with those numbers now. Andie was right, it doesn't matter if they were the exact names of the people in the graves, it matters that we care about who those numbers represent, who they might have been. Because they might have been us.

So there we are, heading back on the country roads, down to the forty-second bottle of beer on the wall, when we see him. The Marlboro Man, hanging out his thumb like it will catch us flying by and we will twirl round and round until we spin to a stop at his boots. His weathered face and mirrored sunglasses just daring us to pass him by, daring us to avoid the flames of passion and the smell of horses and musk and sweat.

Violet says, "Stop! For the love of God stop, you have to stop," and Daphne looks in the rear view mirror at her and says "Are you crazy? I'm not picking up a hitchhiker!" so automatically that she didn't even think about calling Violet crazy. They try not to use that word around us.

The cow says, "What if God was one of us?" and Stuart adds, "Yeah, what about that respecting and helping everyone?" and Kareem laughs. We are a quarter mile past him but I still feel his gaze burning through the back of my head. Violet puts her arms across her chest and pouts. The cow moos loudly. Andie slows down and pulls over.

She puts the van in park and turns around to talk to us. "There is a difference between helping out people you know and picking up a complete stranger, someone you know nothing about. There is a safety concern here that goes beyond being a Good Samaritan."

I look through the rear window of the van. The Marlboro Man has his hands on his hips, waiting to see if we are coming back for him.

"Like the strangers we just spent three hours trying to help?" Stuart asks.

"That's different," Andie says.

"How?" Violet asks, "Because they're just numbers?"

"That's not it at all. Hitchhikers can be dangerous. End of discussion."

I can see how torn she is between doing the right thing, or what she thinks is the right thing, and keeping us safe. She is beyond cute, with her nose scrunched up and her brow furrowed.

She rests her hand on the shift lever, and we wait to see if she is putting it in reverse to pick him up or forward to leave him and his boots and his mustache and biceps and faded jeans behind. Violet crosses her fingers, murmuring, "Please, please, please, he looks so yummy."

Twenty-Seven: Reverse

Maybe it was because she knew what it was like to be left behind. Maybe it was because she wanted to help everyone and not just us. I think it was because she knew we needed to see her help him, just as she was showing us how to help those forgotten numbers buried in the cemetery.

I see the shift lever stop on R. I look back through the rear window and the Marlboro Man gets closer not further. The dust rolls up when Andie stops the van a couple feet short of his boots and faded jeans and smile that has opened up many a bedroom door I am sure.

Kareem opens the sliding door and the Marlboro Man gets in.

"Where you heading, cowboy?" Violet asks, undressing him with her stare that rests mostly on his belt buckle.

"Anywhere with you in it, if that's not too coy," he replies.

"That's not real specific," Andie notes. "Any particular destination?" she asks as she pulls back on to the road. I can tell she is trying not to look at him. Trying not to be instantly charmed by his good looks, his charisma that pours out and hangs heavy in the still air of the van.

He pushes his hat up a little on his head, a few brown curls escaping from underneath it. "Well, ma'am, purt much anyplace we arrive together would keep me from any consternation."

Violet cuddles up to him. "Aw, leave him alone Andie, can't you see he's just happy to be riding instead of walking?" She has a hand half inside his shirt; I see her fingers working on the buttons, trying to expose more of his hairy chest.

"Especially with the ladies with whom I'm talking," the Marlboro Man adds. He puts his arm around Violet and pulls her close and smiles so wide you could jump in.

"What about the guys?" I ask.

And he turns to me and I see my cowgirl eyes mooning at him in the reflection of his sunglasses and he gives a little laugh and says, "I don't think we need them for our little party, pretty brown eyes."

Kareem looks at Pet Shop who looks at Shy Boy who just looks at me. The Marlboro Man pulls out a gun and waves it around and I scream and Violet looks like she is happy to see it.

"Great balls of fire!" moos the cow and the Marlboro Man shoots it. Andie slams on the brakes, almost rolling the van as it slides across the road and into the ditch on the other side. "Jesus Christ!" she shouts. "What the hell is wrong with you?"

"I can't ride in the car with boys and cows, that just won't do," he answers. He opens the sliding door and gestures for Kareem and Pet Shop and Shy Boy and Stuart to get out. "And take this cow that will no longer moo," he adds, gesturing at where I think the invisible cow lies dead.

Pet Shop is crying and Shy Boy is sitting uselessly so Stuart and Kareem drag the cow out to the side of the road. Kareem takes Pet Shop and Shy Boy by the hands and leads them out of the van. The Marlboro Man slides the door shut and he sits with Violet on his lap and she is smiling like she is riding a bucking bronco as Andie pulls away. I look through the rear window at the four guys standing next to the dead invisible cow and then in the rear view mirror at Andie's eyes and she is taking this remarkably well. Considering that her charges have just been kidnapped by the Marlboro Man and he appears to be a black-hatted cowboy and not a white-hatted one. Not to mention that dead cow. How the hell is she going to explain the cow getting shot on her watch?

I am personally not that thrilled with the situation. Sure Violet will keep him entertained for a while, and maybe even Andie will go for his rugged good looks and muscular shoulders. But I don't want any part of it. I don't want a strong man to pick me up and protect me and be my father figure. I don't care if he does smell like horses. I realize that I have to stop the Marlboro Man myself.

Violet says, "Yippee kigh yay!" and Marlboro says, "Let's roll in the hay!" and I realize I have found his kryptonite.

I look at him. His eyes sear a brand in me but I refuse to be part of his posse. I stare right back and say, "Hey, Marlboro Man, do you like oranges?"

The cowboy takes off his mirrored sunglasses and looks at me real mean like and stares but he sees I am not going to say anything more and he loses because there is nothing that rhymes with orange. He puts the glasses back on and gives a little smile like "woman, you just gave away the ranch."

We hit a bump and I am drawn out of my wandering thoughts and I tell Stuart that maybe it was a good idea that Andie kept moving that shift lever past R after all. I would have missed the cow. Andie gives me a quizzical look and I say never mind, I was really just thinking that's all, and she smiles and that's better than some old cowboy anyway.

Twenty-Eight: Return Of The Screech Owl

We decide to walk to the cemetery before supper because we feel really good about helping them and Stuart thinks they should be told that they wouldn't just be names for very much longer. I feel so happy about not picking up the Marlboro Man and having the cow shot that I hold Shy Boy's hand the whole time we are walking out there. I don't even care that I hear the crinkle in his pocket from the picture of Violet's butt.

Stuart goes to each and every tombstone. "And you won't be number three seven dash four three three," he says as he gets to the last one. Violet gives it her now traditional kiss and we all stand in a circle and think about who they were, who they might have been.

"Mary Franklin. Shelley Thurber. Norman Jameson. Peter. Zachariah. Meredith Booker." I recite all of the names I remembered from the library research. "We will remember you. You will be part of us forever."

"Glen. Theodore," Violet adds and I cry a little but they are joyful I love you for thinking of them drops, not I never want to think about them tears. Shy Boy sees how wonderful it all is and pulls my hand toward the front of his pants and I tell him it's not that kind of happy, and he frowns a little but it's okay, I understand he doesn't know the difference. Violet whispers she will help me with him, she will teach me how to make us both happy at the same time and I turn red, but I whisper back thanks Violet I love you.

Pet Shop starts flapping his arms and hooting and I look up just in time to duck as the screech owl has come back and almost flew right into me. It circles a couple times as Pet Shop hoots at it until it finally decides we must be okay and it lands on a branch of the large tree where he and Pet Shop first became friends.

Pet Shop walks slowly up to the base of the tree and the owl shuffles a little on the limb but it stays and Pet Shop looks up and just stares at the owl for the longest time. I think I am going to pass out because if I breathe maybe it will fly away and I don't want it to leave Pet Shop again. The owl lets out a couple loud screeches and turns it head around a few times and flaps it wings. Pet Shop hoots back and twirls around and jumps up and down before letting out this really super loud screech right back at the owl. Well that was a bit much for it I guess because it takes off with that ominous silent glide making me very glad I'm not a field mouse or a rabbit.

Pet Shop turns to face us and all the color has gone from his face — it is whiter than the pearl white skin at the base of Andie's throat.

"What's wrong, Pet Shop?" I ask.

"It's the hedgehog. He has been imprisoned."

Stuart jumps up and down frantically. "Oh God no! Not the hedgehog! We are doomed, doomed I say!"

"Where is he?" I ask Pet Shop.

"The owl said Doctor Martin has captured him. He never did like the hedgehog."

"Doctor Martin doesn't like anyone," Violet says. I have to agree with her on that one. Mean old evil emperor hedgehog capturing bastard. "Well, it's obvious what we have to do."

"You mean –"

"Exactly. I'll give him a blow job so you guys can free the hedgehog."

"Violet, you can't – he'll take you away, you know he will."

Pet Shop looks at Violet, considering the situation. "She's right. Anyway, the hedgehog would be most upset if he thought the doctor had benefited in such a way. No, we have to rescue him without granting Doctor Martin any sexual favors."

Violet pouted, but in the end she admitted the doctor really didn't deserve her services. "Well, if we do have to distract anyone, I call dibs," she states, and we agree that dibs are hers if they come up. No pun intended.

"Plans," Stuart states, "we must make rescue plans. I propose we return to the dorm and strategize. One can never strategize too much, you know. That's why the government controls the food chain, because the farmers fail to meet and strategize."

We look at Pet Shop, it is his hedgehog after all, and with his assent we head back. To strategize.

Twenty-Nine: Strategizing Means Pretty Pictures

Stuart won't let anyone else draw on the paper. Kareem got us crayons and lots of paper but Stuart says it won't work unless he makes all of the pictures because we don't know how to make aerial surveillance maps, whatever those are. So we sit and watch him draw lines and put X's and arrows on the paper. Shy Boy grabs one of the crayons from Stuart. I give Shy Boy a blank sheet so Stuart doesn't get upset, thinking Shy Boy is going to use Stuart's paper.

"Fine," Stuart says, "but we will only use your plan if mine doesn't work. Mine is Plan A, yours is Plan B."

"Attack of the fifty foot woman," moos the cow.

Stuart ponders this option, looks regretful and discounts it. "No, I'm sorry, cow, we don't have one of those. We will have to make do without."

He leans over his aerial surveillance map (I assume that is what he has drawn). "Okay, pay attention now. I can only go over this once. Any more than that and the government might track the thought patterns down and decode them. Repetition is not our friend."

Stuart points at a big X on the map. "That is Doctor Martin's office. That is where I suspect the hedgehog is being interrogated."

Violet points to some of the squares on the map. "What are those?"

"His desk and file cabinets. He might have hidden the hedgehog in a drawer. Or maybe in the cabinet under M. Marsupial."

"Or H?" Pet Shop asks. I guess Pet Shop can spell. I didn't know that, he never guesses at Wheel of Fortune.

"That clever bastard. Yes, we had best look under both M and H."

"You don't show the couch. He could be under the couch."

"How do you know there's a couch in there?" Stuart asks.

Violet replies, "Stuart honey, I know where every couch is in this place."

Stuart accepts her word on that and adds a rectangle for the couch. He colors it in with a blue crayon. He tells Violet it doesn't matter when she informs him that the actual couch is red.

"So how are we getting in?" I ask him. "Doesn't he keep it locked?"

Stuart looks at his aerial surveillance map. He gets real close, nose to paper, looking for the answer. Face still down near the surface of the table, he turns his head to glance sideways at Shy Boy. "Plan B?"

Shy Boy lifts up his paper. There are a couple stick figures holding hands. Violet says, "Aw, isn't that the cutest thing you ever saw." I look closer and see it isn't the stick boy's hand that the stick girl is holding and my face turns red. Shy Boy just grins.

Stuart bangs his head on the table. "No Plan B, we are doomed, doomed I say." Pet Shop starts whimpering.

I take the picture from Shy Boy and give him another piece of paper. "Draw something nice, Shy Boy," I tell him. I'll be embarrassed later, poor Pet Shop is worried about his hedgehog. I put my hand on his shoulder. "It'll be okay, Pet Shop. Listen, how about we ask Andie? She can go into Doctor Martin's office without getting into trouble. I'm sure if we explain it to her she would be glad to help us."

He stops sniffling. "You think so?"

Stuart nods his head. "It's just crazy enough that it might work. Using the angel to inspect the demon's domain."

Violet sighs. "So no bribing anyone, huh? Damn."

Thirty: Slumber Party

It feels good to have someone like Andie we can go to when we are in trouble. I change into my pajamas and crawl into bed and think about how it would have been growing up with Andie. If she was my friend. I snuggle into the blanket and hold onto the pillow and pretend that she is nestled against me and I think warm cozy thoughts not about her naked but about her in pajamas and us giggling about school boys and braiding each other's hair and practicing kissing but not sexual just so we knew how to if a boy ever wanted to kiss us. I fall asleep thinking of her nestled against me.

It is my tenth birthday and Daddy and Mommy let me invite my three bestest friends in the whole world over to spend the night. We are going to dress up and eat popcorn and watch scary movies and tell ghost stories and stay up all night. Whoever goes to sleep first is going to be teased so much so I hope it is Kelly or Jennifer or Liz or Andie. Andie seems different than the others, she is big, but I know she is my best friend even though I thought I just had three, so I hug her when she comes and we run upstairs to my bedroom.

"Liz and Kelly and Jennifer aren't here yet," I tell her.

"That's okay," Andie says. "We can play dress up without them." She takes off her clothes but she doesn't put any more on and then she starts taking my clothes off like Daddy did last night and I start to cry. She says, "Shhhh, don't you want to play, it's a grown up game for my pretty little girl," just like Daddy said and she is putting her fingers in between my legs and I push her away.

"Don't you love me, Daphne?" Andie asks. She reaches for me, pulling me against her warm, full flesh. Rubbing her hands all over my chest. Putting my hands on her body. I cry and say stop and she takes my head in her hands and lifts my face to look at her and says it again. "Don't you love me?"

I look into her eyes and I hear Dad's words echoing through her lips. I stare at her until her face dissolves into his and I scream "How could you do this to me!" and I curse him and beat him until I fall to the floor from exhaustion.

I wake up stark naked. My pajamas are in a rumpled pile across the room. The sheets are soaked in perspiration. That's when it was, I realize. That's when he went from Daddy to Dad. I will never, ever wear pajamas again.

Thirty-One: In A Pissy Mood

Stuart and Pet Shop are all jumpy, eager to start the morning session, whispering about Plan A and B and C. Plan C must be for Andie. Violet is really quiet and Shy Boy keeps trying to hold my hand and I slapped him twice at breakfast, can't they all just leave me alone.

Andie comes in and she is just as lovely and angelic and beautiful and warm and cozy as before and I look at her and think of pajamas and never want to talk to her again. Never want to talk or touch or think about anyone especially *him*, and how could she ever be him, it's not fair she was everything that was pure and now the blackness is in her too. His poison has once again seeped into my waking world.

"We have need of you, my lady," Stuart implores in his best Glen impersonation. "The hedgehog is held in hostile environs, and only you may set him free."

"Herbert, is this true?" she asks.

"Yes, Andie, the screech owl told me," Pet Shop answers. "Doctor Martin has him."

"And you want me to ask the doctor to release him?"

"We think it best," Stuart informs her, "that you use more surreptitious methods than direct communication. It is, after all, an involuntary situation."

"I see." She sits back, tapping her pencil on her notepad. Tap, tap, tap. "Hmmmm." Tap, tap, tap. "I suppose I could have a look around."

"Try M. Oh, and H. He might just be filed under H."

Pet Shop nods, happy Stuart remembered both letters.

"Don't forget to look under the couch," Violet adds. "It's a little squeaky, as couches go, but it might be underneath. If you need any help looking on top of it, let me know."

Andie smiles that gorgeous show of teeth and gloss and the red of the tip of her tongue and it looks nothing like his smile, not in the least bit. But I saw, I know what I saw.

"I will look under M, and H and certainly under the couch. I will leave the door open and instruct the hedgehog that he may escape if he so desires. However," she says, looking intently at Pet Shop, "if he doesn't choose to return you must allow him that. It is, in the end, his choice to be here or not. It is always a choice."

As if it was my choice, as if it is ever a little girl's choice. To trust her daddy. To listen to her daddy. To love her daddy.

"How could you be him?" I suddenly scream and then I am both shouting and crying. She looks startled, how can she be startled when she was there? Tears stream down my face and Shy Boy cowers down in his chair and Stuart and Pet Shop and Violet just watch as I explode. "How the hell can you say I had a choice when you made me love you? It's like saying I chose to have two feet or freckles or to feel like throwing up whenever I smell bacon burning?"

"There is no choice, it's not my fault it's yours, it's your fault, how can you be him?" I sob as she tries to hold me but I push her and start scratching and kicking and biting I don't know who it is I am attacking but it hurts and I hate him, I hate him, I hate him and Sam is pulling me off of her and I feel the needle plunge into my arm and it goes dark.

Thirty-Two: Journey Through Darkness,

Part One

I open my eyes and the world is as dark as it was when they were shut. I see nothing, I hear nothing – I feel nothing. I have no connection with my extremities. Where there should be a brush of air against my skin as I wave my hand before my face there is only tactile emptiness.

I wait in the dark for eternity. It passes. It passes again. Still I wait, alone, beyond sensation, beyond humanity. I wait.

Approximately thirty-seven eons from the end of the universe, I see the dot. A small, insignificant speck of pale light against the backdrop of an infinite blackness. As dim, as weak, as tiny a bit of brightness it is, it still shines like a super nova in contrast to the dark void that I have been in. I rush to it, I cling to it, I call to it, I hunger for it. For anything beyond the depths of despair that entraps me.

I run a thousand marathons and it is an inch closer. I scream oaths into the night and hear nothing as the ebony surrounding me absorbs the sound instantly. I run a thousand more, then another, and after there is nothing left but to run to the speck I find I have approached it. It is within reach. I stretch my hand out to it, grasping it, and I hold it, and it is as if the sun has risen, as if there is life in the universe once again, and the colors rush in and flood my senses and I wake up and she is there. Melissa is there.

Thirty-Three: Journey Through Darkness,

Part Two

Melissa. Everything that should have been. Everything that never was. I fall at her feet and she puts her arms around me and strokes my hair and whispers sweet nothings in my ear, breathing soft, warm breath on my face and my neck and giving me tiny kisses on the top of my head.

Melissa. She was strong and she was beautiful and she was little girl and she was grown-up woman. She was the center of the universe and a cascading meteor with shocking hair and blazing eyes and a sultry dance that no male or female could resist, with pulsating hips and throbbing thighs and curvaceous torso that gyrated around and around and drew one as a moth to a flame.

Melissa who loved Daddy in the way that he wanted. The way that he needed. The way that made him so happy, made him feel so good, made him love her. Melissa who came to me one night and promised that she would be my bestest friend ever.

Melissa who lied. Melissa who never told Mommy, who never stopped Daddy, who only came after, when it was over. Melissa who left when the buckle hit the floor.

I run back, away from the speck that is Melissa, preferring the emptiness, the void, the dark, to the presence of the one who betrayed me when she was all I had left in the world.

Thirty-Four: Journey Through Darkness,

Part Three

I waited in the darkness, facing away from the speck that I knew led only to her. I waited for any other chance, any other path to redemption, than the one that had been offered. I waited in vain.

I turned around. She was closer than I remembered, as if she had approached me, as if she had run for eternity after eternity to find me in this void. I stared at the speck as it grew larger, as the halo of light grew bigger and brighter and once more consumed me.

I was spent, no longer able to resist her pull. No longer able to deny the memories. No longer wanting to avoid the truth.

"Melissa," I hear, and it is not my voice calling the name. "Melissa," he says, "be a good girl for Daddy."

And I want to tell her she doesn't have to do this. That he is wrong. That she is a little girl and pure and wonderful and should be playing with dolls and hopscotch and learning how to match her socks with her belt and not how to cry into her pillow and hide the bruises and pretend it doesn't hurt when you walk.

"Don't you love me?" he asks her and she cries and says "yes, Daddy, I love you," and he doesn't listen to me or to her, he just does it and I want to kill him, I want to kill Daddy and I want her to die so this memory never returns to me again. But he is not kind enough to kill her, no he loves her and cleans her up and tells her he loves her and that this is their little secret. Mommy might not understand how they love each other and I want to scream that it doesn't matter because the bitch will ignore it, she is going to see us and she will pretend it never happened.

But she nods her head and thinks Daddy must really love her if he trusts her with a secret he won't even tell Mommy and maybe Daddy will marry her when she grows up. Because he loves her, he tells her every night. Every night.

He leaves and I go to Melissa and I hold her and tell her it will be okay, that one day Daddy will get really drunk in a bar and hit a telephone pole at sixty miles an hour and Mommy will run off and we will have people who really love us take care of us and help us. People like Glen and Theodore and Stuart and Violet and Pet Shop and Shy Boy and Andie. And I tell her it wasn't real, Andie was never Daddy, she would never ever be Daddy and I hug her and I think maybe it will be all right.

Thirty-Five: Morning After

I wake up and I am in pajamas. I strip them off, throwing them in the wastebasket. I pull on sweat pants and a t-shirt and crawl back into bed.

I stare at the ceiling and it doesn't fall down on me and it doesn't turn into an enormous black hole sucking all the light and life out of the room, it just stays up there all whitewashed and uncracked, and I try to imagine what it would be like to get up and go to breakfast and I throw up all over the bed sheets when I think of the smell of bacon cooking and eggs frying in the kitchen.

Stuart finds me, head against a pillow damp with puke, and says it is okay, no one is watching, no one saw, THEY aren't here. I tell him I don't care, it doesn't matter, nothing matters. Violet joins us and looks at me and starts laughing.

"What's so funny?" I ask, upset that she doesn't see how messed up I am. How can she not see that?

"You, silly girl. Here you are lying in your own puke, feeling sorry for yourself. Let's get you showered off."

So I let her lead me to the showers and she scrubs me over and doesn't even try anything, even when I am all wet and soapy and push against her hand as she rubs the bar over my body. I guess maybe she did see it. She dries me off with a towel that isn't fresh from the dryer but because I know she cares and she understands it feels exactly the same.

We missed breakfast, no big loss when the thought of it makes me want to heave again, but we make it to morning session. I am scared and want to hide under the sheets in my sweats and t-shirt and never come out but Violet makes me go. I don't feel like I have been dried off with a fresh from the dryer towel anymore, I feel like I still have vomit in my hair. I sit down, shaking, not wanting to meet anyone's gaze, not wanting to see what she thinks of me now. Scared she is gone like Melissa.

"Good morning, Daphne," Doctor Martin says. "I hear you had a little excitement yesterday, I would like to talk to you about it."

I lift my head and look around, and Andie isn't there, she has left me to face the evil emperor on my own and I can't blame her, I deserve it.

"Where's Andie?" Stuart asks, "What have you done with her? We are fully capable of rescue missions, it will do no good to lock her away."

Doctor Martin appears more amused than threatened by Stuart's declaration. "I told Doctor MacPherson to take a day off to recover. I wanted to talk to Daphne about it. I felt it might be easier without Doctor MacPherson in the room." He turned to me. "Don't you agree, Daphne, wouldn't it be easier to talk about Doctor – about Andie – without her in the room?"

I don't want to give in to him. I don't want him to see any part of me. I don't want to remember Daddy's face turning into hers.

"Leave her alone," Violet says. "She had a rough night."

"No rougher than Doctor MacPherson's, I'm sure."

"Come on, Doc, lay off. If you want to get into anything how about you and me go make that couch of yours squeak."

Sam edges nearer. I think he got yelled at last time when he let Violet get close enough to latch on to Doctor Martin. Violet sees him. "Relax, Sam, it was a friendly invitation. If Doc here isn't interested, maybe you would like to take his place?" She runs her hand down his chest. He grabs her by the wrists before she can do anything more enticing.

"Sorry, honey, why don't you take a seat and talk to the doctor?" He pushes her back down onto the chair before releasing her arms.

She crosses her arms. "What's a girl got to do to get laid around here anyway?"

Sam laughs but Doctor Martin's face remains stoic. "Daphne, do you remember what you did yesterday? When you were talking to Andie? Can you tell me what happened?"

He is persistent; I'll give him that. I stare at him. He stares back. I wonder what it would be like to gouge out his eyes with my fingers, but figure that Sam would have me down on the floor with my arms pinned back and a knee in the small of my back before I could sink my thumbs into the soft squishy orbs.

Seconds turn into minutes turn into hours. Does he sense my confidence? Does he somehow know that just last night I stared into deepest black for infinity? That seconds or minutes or hours mean nothing to one who was cast into the void for eternity? He must, for it is he who breaks first.

He gets up; his bones crack from the long period of inactivity. He walks out of the room without a word to any of us. After the door shuts, sealing him out more than us in, Stuart giggles. Sam pulls me out of the chair. He is a little grabby, in my opinion. Violet tells him to lay off of me, if he wants a little action to see her and Sam gives her a look like she just might get what she's asking for one of these days. Pow, to the moon, I think.

Thirty-Six: Shy Boy Gets A Kiss

It is a little harder to slip past Sam this time, but we eventually lose him and head out to the cemetery. The sky is full of brooding storm clouds. I expect the downpour will start about the time we get there. If it started sooner we would turn away and if it started later then it wouldn't matter, we would already be on our way back.

Shy Boy and Pet Shop are with us. I don't know why they missed the morning session. I ask Pet Shop and he says he was working on Plan C and hoping that Andie comes back tomorrow so she can save the hedgehog. At the mention of Andie the conversation dies and I walk silently. Shy Boy keeps sneaking glances at me and the cow says "Somebody's watching me" and Stuart looks around for flying saucers or spies or who knows what. I blush and keep walking.

Violet crowds me and I bump into Shy Boy and he pretends it wasn't on purpose. He bumps back into me a couple steps later and I give him a teeny smile and his face lights up, and I don't even notice the spittle dripping down the side of his chin. It is so cute that a little contact can change his world like it does. I guess a little contact can change mine as easily.

I refrain from clasping his hand although it is offered, but it does not dampen his spirits and the air is crisper and we walk more rapidly as if we know that something magical is waiting for us at the cemetery.

The grass is still overgrown and the fence is still broken down and there are still scraps of tin foil scattered about. The tombstones still bear only numbers and single dates as indication of the dead beneath them. The thunderclouds still hang heavy in the air with their threat of watery assault. Doctor Martin is still a bastard, and I still know that I hurt Andie. Despite all of that, maybe because of all that, I stand at the base of the big tree and take Shy Boy's hand and I dance and I laugh and I tell them all that I love them.

The rain comes, and though it is cold we do not leave. It pelts us and we find shelter under the tree. Our clothes are heavy and Violet says let's take them off and we do. It is cold but we are sweating and Shy Boy reaches for me and I reach for him and we kiss. A tender, walking you home from the movies only a little bit late and Dad please don't turn on the porch light we are just saying good night kiss. It is every kiss I never got and it makes me feel like I can still call him Daddy not Dad and I want it to last forever.

Violet is watching us and I know she wants me to do more than kiss Shy Boy but I push her out of my thoughts and only think of innocence. As I breathe him in and he breathes me in, as we kiss naked in the rain, I tell him this is all I have, this is all I can do. Even though he is ready for more, that is obvious as I feel his hardness against my thigh. I hug him because he isn't rocking forward, he isn't rubbing himself on me, he isn't forcing my legs apart and he isn't like *him* at all. And I cry on his shoulder and the rain comes down and Violet watches us not make love and Pet Shop says he is cold and so we put on our clothes and go back.

Sam yells at us when he sees the sorry state we are in and tells us all to go take showers and that he better not catch us running outside in a storm again or else. Violet says "or else what" and pats Sam on the butt and he just scowls.

Thirty-Seven: Plan C

It is lights out time and I get in my not-pajamas sleeping sweats and t-shirt and think about Shy Boy and Andie. I want to tell her I am sorry, that I know it wasn't her and I hope she is back tomorrow.

I am almost asleep when Stuart startles me. "Daphne," he whispers, "Daphne, get up. It's time. Plan C has started."

"What? I thought Andie was –"

"That's exactly what everyone was supposed to think. No, the real Plan C is a closely held secret, known only to myself, Pet Shop, the cow and maybe Shy Boy. I can never tell when he is listening."

"Well, I knew, too," Violet says. Good thing it's my room and nobody is supposed to be here at night. Might as well have roll call.

Stuart is a bit miffed at everyone (but me) knowing his secret plan. Violet tells him she didn't know exactly when he was doing it so they couldn't have read her mind and spoiled it and he accepts that and says the plan is still a go.

"We are going to have to break Pet Shop and Shy Boy out next. I don't think they will make it on their own." Stuart leads us down the corridor and we see Sam sleeping in a chair. I guess he is on night duty this week. We tiptoe by Sam and into the wing where Pet Shop and Shy Boy sleep. I've never been in their rooms but Violet says they are all the same and I don't doubt that she's been in most of the rooms if not beds in this building.

We get Shy Boy first because we know he won't make any noise. "He'll be the perfect look out man," Stuart says, "quiet as a mouse." I decide not to point out that he will be just as quiet if he sees anyone coming, which won't give us a lot of warning. I like having him with us, who cares if we get caught. He is so sleepy I muss up his hair and he smiles. I'm not sure if he knows this isn't a dream so I give him a quick kiss so he will think it is a good dream and not a scary one.

Stuart slinks down the hallway to Pet Shop's room. He darts back and forth, hiding in doorways and waving us forward when it is safe to proceed. He isn't amused when Violet suggests we skip and sing show tunes. "They would never suspect us if we were doing that," she states, and she may be right but I agree with Stuart that perhaps a silent approach would be best.

Pet Shop is excited when we get to his room. "I asked the cow if he could find a rooster to make sure I woke up on time but he said they only give wake up calls at dawn and it wouldn't help. So I just stayed up and counted sheep."

"You have sheep, too?" I ask.

Pet Shop looks at me in astonishment. "Don't be silly. Whoever heard of invisible sheep?"

We proceeded down the hall and to the staff offices. Arriving at Doctor Martin's office, we were confronted with our first major obstacle. The door was locked. "How could he have known?" Stuart asked. "The one day we execute Plan C and he locks his door."

"I think he locks it every day," I tell him.

"That diabolical fiend. To enact a habit such as that just so Plan C could be foiled at some indeterminate point in time. I salute your manic genius, Doctor Martin, as I curse its ingenuity."

"Where's that monkey when you need him?" Pet Shop asks. He points up at the top of the door. There is one of those small windows above it. "The monkey could go through the transom and unlock the door for us." I guess those small windows are transoms. Damn but Pet Shop is smarter than I gave him credit for.

"Well," Violet says, "lacking a monkey I guess I can get through that. I've been in tighter places. Come on, Pet Shop, give me a boost."

Violet slides through the transom and lands with a thump on the other side. She unlocks the door. Stuart tells Shy Boy to stand watch and the rest of us enter the office.

"Here little hedgehog, here buddy, it's okay, we're here to save you from the mean old doctor," Pet Shop calls. Stuart heads for the filing cabinet.

"Come out, come out wherever you are," entreats the cow. I figure he has as much chance as any of us at spotting the hedgehog, being of the invisible variety himself.

Stuart shuts the drawer of the filing cabinet. "Where can he be?"

The couch starts squeaking as Violet bounces up and down on it. "Told you it squeaked," she says. "I checked — he's not under here."

Stuart paces back and forth. "He's not under M, he's not under the couch…"

"You fool, you forgot about checking H!" Pet Shop races to the filing cabinet, opens the drawer.

"Rescue me," we hear crooning from Pet Shop's arms. "Rescue me."

"Success!" Stuart exclaims.

"What the hell is going on in here?" The booming voice of Sam rains on our parade. He has Shy Boy by the arm, dragging him into the office. I guess it isn't going to be a happy dream for Shy Boy after all.

Violet pulls Pet Shop onto the couch. He is very surprised and tries to get up but she grabs onto him and keeps him on top of her. "We're just trying out the couch, Sammy. We heard it was the best place in the whole building. Want to give it a try after we're done?"

"There'll be none of that in here. Now go on, all of you, back to your rooms. You are going to catch it from Doctor Martin when he hears about this."

Violet lets Pet Shop get up off of her and slides over to Sam. She brushes her hand against his cheek, running her fingers through his hair, pushing her chest up against his. "Now Sam," she says, "you don't want to tell mean old Doc about this, do you?"

"I don't?" He is mesmerized, entranced, totally looking at her boobs pressed against his chest.

She continues to stroke his hair, rubbing his ear lobes between her fingers, leaning against him. "No, of course you don't. We wouldn't want him to know how a bunch of us were able to slip past you and break into his office, now would we? We wouldn't want our friend Sam to get in trouble over that. Not when we can just all go back and behave and sleep real quiet, right?"

Sam absorbs this. Violet is right, I think at him, trying to sway him to see her logic. She gives him one last caress, her hand trailing down his chest, circling his waist, cupping his butt briefly before she puts a finger to his lips. "Shhhh, we'll just be tiptoeing back to bed. You be a dear and go back to sleep yourself."

Violet leads us back to our rooms. I give Shy Boy another quick peck on the cheek so he knows I don't blame him for not warning us about Sam. It looked like Pet Shop wanted one too but I ignored him. He's got the hedgehog back; he doesn't need any loving from me. I ask Violet if she wants to sleep, just sleep I tell her, and she says that maybe it would be best if she didn't. She wanted to stay up and keep an eye out for Sam, just in case. I say okay and slide under the sheets and go back to thinking about Shy Boy and Andie and how Violet is sometimes my favorite person even when she is sleeping around with anything that moves.

I hear the door open and I can feel *him* standing there, watching me and I keep my eyes closed, and I know if I can stay asleep, then before I know it morning will come. I wait in the darkness and pray that he will go away. That when I open my eyes it will be morning and I will have made it through the night unscathed. The door closes and I bite my lip until I hear the footsteps receding down the hall instead of approaching the bed. I keep my eyes closed just in case and when I open them next it is morning and I did make it and I thank Violet for standing guard. She hugs me and says it's no big deal but I owe her one and pretty soon she is going to want a favor from me. Anything, I tell her, but I'm not certain if I mean it. What could she need from me that she hasn't taken already?

Thirty-Eight: Andie's Return

We eat breakfast and I am feeling so much better that I even eat some eggs. No bacon, it isn't that good but still the eggs are okay and not runny and I don't feel like puking after I eat them. Shy Boy's eyes are bright and he isn't drooling and I don't know if I have ever seen him look so alive and he smiles at me and I guess it was a happy dream for him after all. Violet even smiles at him and then at me, and she says softly so only I can hear, "Isn't Shy Boy looking hot today?" I just give her a little nod. I don't even blush, I just accept that I can think he looks hot and that Violet knows it and it is okay.

"It's a beautiful day in the neighborhood," the hedgehog tells us. Pet Shop is beaming and Stuart is also on top of the world. I think this is the first time one of his top secret covert missions actually came off without a hitch. Except for getting caught by Sam, but Violet took care of that and the hedgehog was rescued from Doctor Martin and no blood was shed so I would still call it a success.

We go to morning session and I am afraid to look, I don't want another session with Doctor Martin but it would be worse if Andie was there and hated me. If she didn't forgive me. If she wasn't Andie anymore.

We all sit down and Shy Boy scoots his chair closer to me and I still don't blush. Kareem is watching us today and at least that part of the session is better than before. The door opens and it isn't Doctor Martin, it is Andie and she is wearing the sweater that wants to roll in leaves and walk hand in hand and she sees I am there and she smiles and I know it is the real Andie and she doesn't hate me.

"Good morning, everyone," she says, and I say "Good morning, Andie" back to her and she is still smiling and her eyes are still Bambi-brown and she still smells of coffee and I know I will always love her.

"Good morning, Vietnam," sings the hedgehog, and Andie raises her eyebrows at Pet Shop.

"We rescued him!" Pet Shop tells her.

Stuart places his finger on his lips, "Shhhh, we might need to use Plan C again, you know."

Andie has a puzzled look on her face but she can tell just how gosh-darned happy Pet Shop and Stuart are and she lets it alone. Doctor Martin would have hammered them about any secrets until it wasn't a good day anymore. Andie is so different from Doctor Martin.

"Well, Herbert, I am glad your friend is back. Remember what I told you before, though – there might be a day when he leaves again, and that is his choice. Sometimes our friends have to go to other places, sometimes places we can't follow them to. That's part of life."

I soak in the words. She goes on with Pet Shop and Stuart about letting the animals make their own choice but I am still thinking about friends going to other places. Leaving. Abandoning.

I reach for her; she lets me take her hand. "Don't leave, Andie. Please don't leave me."

"Oh, Daphne, I'm not leaving. I have no plans to do anything but stay here and help all of you. To get to know you better. There may come a day when you decide it is time to leave, but that will be your choice. Not mine."

Shy Boy starts at these words, almost falling out of his chair. Andie looks at him, "What's wrong, Gordon?"

He keeps his head down, almost shrinks as he sits in the chair. "Gordon, please tell me, what is it?"

He shakes his head "no," and I can see the surprise in Andie's face that she got that much of a response out of him. She writes something down on her notepad. I have never seen her do anything but doodle or tap her pencil on it before.

"If you don't want to talk about it right now that's okay."

I scoot over a little in my chair, so my leg is just barely touching his. He feels the contact, stops shaking his head, settles down. It feels nice when he scoots a little toward me, increasing the pressure of leg upon leg.

I gather my courage and clear my throat to get Andie's attention. "Andie, are you... okay?"

She clasps my hand. "I'm fine Daphne. I know it gets emotional in here. I know sometimes we do things we don't mean to."

"I'm so sorry, I didn't want to hurt you. It was *him*, not you."

"Who was it, Daphne? Who hurt you?"

The words hang there. I've been asked them a million times. I know she knows what happened, most of it anyway. They all do. But they still want me to say it. To repeat the worst events of my life, over and over. As if the nightmares weren't enough to remind me. As if telling the story would make the world a safer place where little girls didn't love their daddies during the day and fear them at night.

But this is Andie. This is the one who cares. The one who helped Glen and Theodore and who loves me. I know she loves me. I close my eyes, I squeeze her hand, and I tell her the dreams.

I tell her about hiding in closets. I tell her about crying into pillows. I tell her about bacon and newspapers in the morning. I tell her about Daddy becoming Dad and Mommy becoming Mom. I tell her about my dad's face dissolving into hers and she holds me and rocks me and I cry on her shoulder and she still loves me, she doesn't think I am a worthless or evil little girl who made my daddy do those things.

I don't tell her about her undressing me. I don't tell her about loving her, about how she smells, how the curl of hair around her ears makes me feel like dancing. I don't tell her about Melissa. I only tell her all the things she already knows but it still feels good and if she accepts these things about me then maybe someday I can tell her the rest of them too.

Thirty-Nine: Arts And Crafts

We are finishing lunch when Andie comes to our table. "Hey, how would you all like to work on our project this afternoon?"

She asks this like we would ever choose to do anything other than be with her. As if any sentence with the word project would be anything other than an automatic "pick me" from Stuart. As if we didn't sit around and try to figure out ways to spend more time with her.

"I guess that would be okay," Violet says. "I don't have anyone – I mean anything scheduled right now."

Andie ignores the innuendo and smiles and says "Great" and we put our lunch trays up and follow her to the art room.

We sit down and Andie unloads the box that Kareem was carrying for her. She gives us each several cardboard rectangles.

"It is going to be very difficult to draw aerial surveillance maps on these," Stuart informs her. "I need a full sheet of paper to detail where the guard posts are."

"These aren't for maps, Stuart. What we are going to do is write the names that we discovered for the people in the cemetery. We can add drawings on the cards also, like flowers or rainbows or anything we think the person might have liked."

"Can I draw animals?"

"Yes, Herbert, but we want to be able to see them, so only draw visible ones."

"How about an orgy?"

"Let's try to draw things that are okay for kids to see, alright?"

Violet pouts. "Fine."

"There is a flaw in your plan. We have observed rain in the cemetery. I do not believe these cards will be able to withstand the rain. They can't just take off their clothes like we can."

For a moment Andie looks like she is going to ask Stuart about the taking off clothes part, but she shakes her head slightly, apparently judging it best to just address his concern. "The cards won't be out there. After we have them all prepared, Kareem is going to take them to an engraver for us. The engraver will take our cards and use them to create metal copies that we can attach to a plaque. We will put the plaque in the cemetery so everyone can see their names and your drawings."

"As long as the plaque is rust-resistant."

"I'll make sure it is. Now, shall we start?"

It's interesting, trying to decide what to draw on the cards. What would Shelly Thurber want on her card? A rose? A cat? I think about her, try to imagine living here back when she did, when they gave you a number and took away your name. I go with the cat. Something to curl up with her and purr when she pets it and make her feel special and wanted and needed. A cat, that should work just fine.

Norman Jameson? A jack-in-the-box. He can wind it up whenever he is sad and it will pop up and surprise him and he can laugh. I'm not sure if I draw it very well but I am sure he will understand.

I peek over at Pet Shop's card. It looks like he is drawing the whole zoo on his. I see a tiger and an elephant and a zebra. His drawing looks better than mine. If I ever get a card I want him to make it. Except maybe without the tiger.

Shy Boy has added a couple stick figures to his card. I remember the picture he drew for me and I wait to see what the girl stick figure is holding on to. It ends up being the boy stick figure's hand and I pat his hand for behaving. He looks at me and I don't know if something got in his eye but I think he winked! He goes back to drawing and I sit there and wonder about how Shy Boy is changing. He isn't so shy anymore.

Violet has taken a card and has colored the entire thing black. She shows it to Andie. "See, I censored the parts the kids weren't supposed to see."

"Thank you Violet, that's a fine job."

I go back to the card for Norman Jameson and decide that it would be better if the jack-in-the-box was out of the box. Because it kind of looks like just a box, sitting there closed. I ask Andie for another card and try it again.

We aren't the fastest artists, and Andie has to help us with most of the spelling. Except Pet Shop, he is a good speller. We get about a dozen done before suppertime (not counting Violet's which I think Andie threw away). Andie tells us we can finish up tomorrow, so we help her pack up the cards and markers back into the box.

Forty: Never Been Kissed

It is night, and I think about Shy Boy more than Andie. It was great that Andie is back and that she still loves us but it was really weird when Shy Boy winked at me. I wonder if I am falling for the silly boy and what would it be like if I was with him. Really with him. Like he wants. I hug my pillow and kiss it and pretend it is Shy Boy and it is different with Shy Boy than it is with Violet, but it isn't like it was with *him*, no *he* never kissed me, *he* was all hands and fingers and penis. Forcing and shoving and thrusting and pain.

I think about boys and kisses and then I am fourteen and I want to go to the movies with Jennifer and Mom says okay. It is an early show so we will be back before dark, I tell her, and she gives me an extra five dollars so I can have popcorn and candy and a drink and not just a movie.

"Your mom's the greatest," Jennifer says as we walk to the theater. "My mom never gives me anything."

I don't say "Yeah, but she turns up the TV whenever Dad rapes me in the laundry room." I don't say that because I am fourteen and I am with my girlfriend and we are going to the movies just like any two girls in the world. Instead I say, "Yeah, she's pretty cool," and smile and we chew bubble gum and talk about who is the cutest boy in the ninth grade and I say Peter Wilkins and she says Justin Gore and I say "Ew, gross" and we laugh and giggle all the way to the theater.

Peter and Justin are both at the movie. They sit behind us and pull on our hair and say stuff about us that we pretend we can't hear even though they know we can. I think somebody must have told them we liked them. They are funny and obnoxious and the cutest boys in the ninth grade. And they are teasing us!

Halfway through the movie they get up. Jennifer and I look at each other, wondering what we did to them, were we too funny or too serious or too ugly? Then they are sitting next to us one on each side of us, they didn't leave they changed seats, oh my God, what do we do now?

They are talking to us — not about us! — now, and it isn't five minutes before they both do the fake yawn and it is so obvious but Jennifer and I sit there, afraid to move a muscle as their arms slowly descend to rest on the back of the seats. I see Jennifer snuggle in to rest her head on Justin's shoulder but I am scared, I don't know if I should. I sense Peter waiting for me to settle in against him and I take a deep breath and exhale and tell myself as soon as I finish exhaling I am going to do it, I am going to lean against him and before I can chicken out I do, oh my God, I am leaning against him now.

I don't know if it is Peter or me or both of us but somebody sure is trembling. We sit there, staring straight at the movie for at least ten minutes, not knowing what to do next. I guess Jennifer and Justin figured it out first because next thing you know they are making out like a couple of old pros. My heart starts pounding, I know Peter wants to make out and I see him turn his head and he leans down and he tilts to one side so I can lean up and tilt my head to the other side. I close my eyes as his lips descend toward my own.

In my mind I hear a belt buckle hit the floor and I know what he wants to do to me and I shut it out I shut it all out and then it all goes dark. A powerful voice rings out into the theater and next thing I know I am sitting at home wrapped up in a blanket. A policeman is there and says that Peter needed thirteen stitches and then Dad says he is going to kill the little bastard for laying a hand on his little girl and I laugh hysterically and can't stop and finally Mom shouts at him to get the hell out of the room. Then they took me away. Away from peeing my pants when I was walking down a dark hallway and heard footsteps behind me. Away from screaming in my pillow as he thrust over and over until his release shot into me. Away from morning newspapers and burnt bacon.

It is morning once more. I struggle to remember what Peter Wilkins even looked like. He definitely wasn't as cute as

Shy Boy. Anyway, I've already kissed Shy Boy. It was a little scary but he is different, he hasn't made me do anything except think about him and I enjoy thinking about him. Thinking about what it might be like. To be with him. To have him in me because I want him not because he forces it. Because I love him for how he really is and not who he is supposed to be. But I am still scared.

I talk to Violet before breakfast. About Shy Boy. About Peter Wilkins. About being scared and never kissing a boy when I was fourteen. She understands all of it.

"Daphne, dear, don't you worry about a thing. Shy Boy will handle all the mechanics, you just need to lie back and enjoy the ride. You care enough about him that it shouldn't be a rough one – I know he gets you going, I can see the look in your eyes when you're watching him. It won't be anything like it was with – *him.*"

"But I liked Peter Wilkins, too. I really did. I don't want to hurt Shy Boy. I'm terrified that we're going to start, you know, doing it, and I'll freak out."

Violet drew her hand across my lips. "Hush now, Daphne. It will be okay – Violet will take care of it for you. Leave everything to me. I'll make sure you know what you're doing. Trust me, I know how to make it enjoyable for everyone. Very enjoyable. Shy Boy will be – well, harder than putty in your hands, when we're done with him."

Forty-One: Feeding The Screech Owl

Pet Shop asks everybody to get extra toast at breakfast. He wants to take it out to the cemetery before morning session and leave it for his friend the screech owl. Stuart eagerly grabs half a loaf's worth. Always ready to assist in anything that bears resemblance to a plan. And stealing from "the man," that's just a bonus.

Shy Boy takes my hand as we walk out to the cemetery. Not in a territorial, you "must" way, but more of a wouldn't it be nice if we held hands way. The kind that allows me to let him hold on. Violet notices but doesn't do anything to embarrass me. Sometimes she surprises me.

"Walking on sunshine," the hedgehog says, and even if it is a little cloudy it doesn't look like it will rain – maybe I want it to rain and run naked through the woods chasing Shy Boy? – but it feels like sunshine. Shy Boy's hand in mine is like a little miniature furnace, I feel his heat and it goes up my arm and into my chest and I hum snappy silly pop songs along with the hedgehog.

We arrive at the cemetery and Violet kisses three seven dash four three three hello and Stuart smiles because he knows it won't be long before there is more than a number and a date there. Pet Shop gathers everybody's toast and starts spreading it around the cemetery.

I sit at the base of the big tree and Shy Boy sits next to me and I lean over to him and he leans over to me. I tilt my head to the side and he does the same. I don't close my eyes for fear the darkness will envelop me. I watch his lips descend and when they reach mine it is more than the kiss we had before but it doesn't consume me and it doesn't make me freak out and he keeps his hands to himself and I am fourteen again and being kissed for the first time.

I lean back against the tree and look up in the branches where Pet Shop is hiding pieces of toast. Shy Boy just sits there not demanding not asking not needing anything and I wait and he doesn't change. He still sits there and I hold his hand and I think it must have been wonderful to feel like this at fourteen. To think that this is what it was all about and not worry about what will happen tonight when the lights go out and the door creaks open and the footsteps cross the bedroom and the belt buckle hits the floor. This is how it should have been, I think, and I kiss Shy Boy again and he still doesn't ask for anything more than what I offer.

Pet Shop starts flapping his arms and screeching, no doubt broadcasting in owl speech the bounty of toast awaiting his feathered friend. We wait for a little while but the screech owl must not have heard. "He'll find it, Pet Shop," Stuart tells him. "It was a good plan."

We head back. Pet Shop keeps looking over his shoulder to see if the owl is flying by. I keep looking at Shy Boy.

Forty-Two: Andie Tells Us Another Story

We get to session and Andie is already there. She is sitting down, scribbling on her notepad. The box of cards and markers isn't around so I guess we will do that in the afternoon.

We sit down and Andie keeps scribbling on her notepad. I try to see what she is writing but the notepad is angled away from me so I can't tell.

So we sit and wait because we never start. Andie always starts with a "good morning." Not us. Andie. But she doesn't. She just sits there writing away and not showing us what she is writing and not greeting us good morning and acting like we aren't even in the room.

As expected, Violet breaks the silence. Too much time with too little attention paid to her, I knew she couldn't stay quiet for much longer.

"So, darling," she says, "you writing me a love letter?"

Andie pushes her glasses back up her nose and I forget all about whatever it was she was writing. A simple movement, a flash of eyes, a hint of a smile, and I am hers even if Shy Boy is perfect today. It doesn't mean I don't care about him but there is something about Andie that draws me in, like she is a deep well of purity that I need to drink of to be whole.

"Sorry, Violet, didn't mean to keep you waiting. No, it's not a love letter, to answer your question. I was just checking on some of my notes, had some thoughts I wanted to get down, before we began our session today." She puts the notepad down, smiles and says, "Good morning, everyone." And I know it isn't going to be a weird world turned upside down session like I was worried it could have been.

"Good morning," she says, and we know that she cares, that the evil emperor is not there today, that we can tell her anything we want to and she won't hate us or be scared of us or lock us away. "Who wants to start?"

I stir on my chair and she looks my way and I am as surprised as she is that I want to be the first today. "Daphne?"

"I was just wondering. Curious. Sort of. If you ever..."

"Ever what?"

"Jumped off the Eiffel Tower?" Stuart asks.

"Joined the Mile High Club?"

"Skated backwards?"

"Ate ants alongside an aardvark?"

"Appeared on Wheel of Fortune?"

"Enough with the guesses," Andie quiets them. "Daphne, go on, you can ask me anything you want."

I plunge in. "Did you ever love anyone? I mean, I know you were married and all, but he was a jerk and so I don't think you really loved him if that was how he turned out. Did you ever love anyone else?"

Andie sits back, removes her glasses, and takes a deep breath. "Wow. That's a question, all right."

"You said anything," Pet Shop reminds her.

"I guess I did." She puts her glasses back on, takes them off again and plays with them a little more. We sit patiently, waiting for her answer.

"Yes – no – maybe..." Andie says, apparently having as hard a time answering the question as I did asking it.

We wait but she just sits there, lost in thought.

"Could you elaborate?" Violet asks. "Feel free to go into graphic details if that gets you in the mood."

"Behave, Violet," I instruct her. "Andie, please tell us more."

Andie stops fidgeting with her glasses. "It happened a couple years ago. It was after I left my husband. I had taken another internship and there was a young man working at the same hospital. We were both so busy with work and classes that we hardly had time for each other. Maybe that's why we called it love, because we managed to fall in it despite hardly ever seeing each other."

Andie takes a deep breath and continues. "He was handsome and sweet and would have been just the type to bring home to meet your parents, except of course I didn't. I was scared they might like him and they were so far off on the last one I really didn't want their approval. And neither of us were looking for marriage, we were both just looking for companionship, for someone to hold onto when we came home exhausted from another shift. Someone who understood what we were doing and didn't need an explanation when we were too tired to make love or clean the carpets or talk about where to go to dinner."

"But when we weren't too tired — Lord, we had fun then." She gives a sad, bittersweet smile that reflected all the happiness that was and could have been. "Whether it was dancing in the moonlight, or walking in the park, or making love like it was the first time or might be the last time we ever had a chance to. It was everything I ever wanted and never had to fight for, it was all so easy. I guess in the end it was too easy."

"The end?" I ask, the sound barely audible, knowing that she was here so it had to end but trying to believe in it enough that maybe it was still there for her. Hoping maybe she would give a wink, letting me in on the big secret that this man was still living with her, that the fairy tale went on happily ever after.

"Yes, it ended. And not badly or noisily or with hatred or anger. It ended as easily as it had begun. Our shifts changed, our internships were over, opportunities arose in different cities. And though we had been in love we were never committed and our routines developed without each other as quickly as they had been established in unison."

I reach for her to hold her and although I think it comforts me more than her I feel her hug me a little tighter than before. So I hug back harder, wanting her to know that this one is for her, that I am giving it not taking it. That she is still loved.

Forty-Three: Finishing The Tags

In the afternoon Andie and Kareem again lead us into the art room. She hands out more blank cards. I get another name from her to put on my card. It is Felix. Felix doesn't have a last name, and I am torn between either giving him one or drawing an extra large cat on it. But then the people visiting the cemetery might think Felix really was a cat and that wouldn't be fair to him.

"Andie, I need a last name for Felix, can I give him one?"

"Sure Daphne, I think he would like that. Whatever you want." Andie looks at Violet, answering the question before it is asked. "Violet, no body parts for last names."

"Not even asshole?"

"No."

Violet hmmphs. "Guess we aren't making any for Doc Martin then."

Stuart giggles, even Andie laughs. "Just keep them clean, please."

Shy Boy hands his first finished card to Andie and takes another one. She sits there, staring at it. I lean over to see if he has the stick girl grabbing onto something inappropriate and am taken aback. His drawing is detailed and the people look like people and he stayed in all the lines.

"Gordon, this is wonderful," Andie tells him. "You've been holding back on us. Samantha's plate is going to be very special with this engraved on it."

He smiles and his face turns a little flushed from all the attention. He goes back to drawing on the next card and I see Andie sneak off to the other table and she is writing in her notepad again.

I look at my card, try to think what I would be if I was Felix's last name, and it comes to me: Potato. I write it on the card and draw some French fries and a potato with big eyes. I don't show it to Stuart because he might think the eyes were looking at him.

Violet has drawn another orgy scene on her card. When she finishes she proceeds to take the black marker and darken it out completely. "Poor little kids, the things they could learn if they would let me show them." She grabs another card and repeats the process. When she is done, she has three very ornately drawn orgy scenes that you can't see anything of because they are all blacked out.

Shy Boy's cards are definitely the featured attraction from our little art show. He only drew two but they look like they should be framed and hanging on the wall of a museum.

Andie gathers them all up. She has a couple she drew but she didn't show them to us – I am guessing she is probably a better artist than I am but not as good as Shy Boy.

"When are we going to put these in the cemetery?" I ask Andie.

"Kareem will take them to the engraver today. He should have the plates all done and the plaque ready in a couple days."

"Can he be trusted?"

"Sure I can," Kareem says, but he is smiling to show he didn't take the remark personally.

"Not you, Kareem," I explain. "Stuart means the engraver."

Andie nods. "I've known the engraver for years – that's why he is getting them finished for us so quickly. He displays no signs of governmental influence."

"I'm a believer," says the hedgehog, instantly alleviating Stuart's concern.

"Guess that seals it," Andie says. "We will trust the engraver."

Forty-Four: *Spin That Wheel*

Couch time again. Shy Boy has his arm around me, and I am leaning into his shoulder, and I don't have flashbacks of Peter Wilkins, I don't curl my hand into a fist and knock out three teeth and require him to have thirteen stitches. I just lean into him and smell him and he smells good, not coffee or leaves like Andie but not cigars and aftershave like *him* but just like Shy Boy should smell like. A lot less like cabbage than he used to.

"LESBIAN LICKING IN SHOWER STALLS," Violet shouts at the TV.

I glance at the puzzle. "That's only five words, there are supposed to be six."

"Fine.   LESBIAN LICKING IN THE SHOWER STALLS."

Shy Boy pulls the blanket further up until it covers us both from the chest down. I don't think much of it until his other arm, the one that isn't curled behind my head, starts to slide under the blanket. I move my hand to intercept it, to hold hands like I think he wants. But that's not what he wants. His hand glides over mine, giving it a gentle caress but continuing, moving past until it is aligned with my belly button. And I am not breathing, I am staring at the letters on the screen and I am scared.

He keeps his hand flat, the palm presses against my belly, and it feels warm as it rests against my skin. And I keep my head nestled in the eave of his shoulder and I feel his moist exhale on my cheek and I hear his heart pounding unless that is my own so loud it must be echoing off of the walls.

His hand inches higher, flesh on flesh. Soon it will be on my right breast, and then he will want the left one, too, and God only knows how long after that before he heads south. I like Shy Boy, I really do, but I am so scared and I don't know what to do. I don't know how to be with a boy when I want to be with him, I don't know what is supposed to feel good and what isn't and when it is love and when it is rape.

I grab his arm and pull it from under my shirt. I stand up, the blanket dropping on the floor. "I'm sorry, Shy Boy, I'm sorry," I tell him before running off to my room.

Kareem follows me. I am sobbing into my pillow when I hear him cross the room.

"Are you okay, Daphne? Was Gordon doing anything to you?" he asks.

I try to hold the tears in, to calm down enough to talk to Kareem.

"No, he wasn't doing anything, it's just, it's just that I like him and I don't know how to like him. I don't know how to be with him. I'm scared, Kareem, I don't know how to love."

He holds me, rocking me until I calm down. "Daphne, no one knows how to love. Not you, not me, not Gordon. Nobody. We all just fake it. What really matters is that we respect each other's rules, that we don't hurt anyone else. Then, when we try it with people we love, it doesn't really matter if it's awkward or difficult. Because if he loves you and you love him then all the other stuff just washes away."

I cling to him, to his kindness, to his empathy. "Can you… teach me?"

He moves a little away from me on the bed. "Daphne, I care about you, I do. But I am not in love with you, and I can't do that with you."

"I understand, Kareem. You're just so nice I thought I would ask."

He hugs me good night and says he will tell the others I am okay and wishes me sweet dreams. He is so good. And maybe gay.

Violet visits me a little later, before I am asleep. She crawls under the covers with me and it is nice to have someone I am used to there. Someone who is soft not hard. Who is gentle not forceful. Who loves me not uses me. I tell her about Kareem and she gives me a little smile.

"Darling, don't take it personally. I mean, if he could resist me…"

"Yeah, I know. He's just so nice, I thought maybe it would help me let Shy Boy, you know, be with me."

She guides my hand down between my legs. "You mean, be with you here?"

I tell her yes.

"Remember that favor you owe me?" she asks, her hand still pressing on mine, pushing it back and forth. I don't say a word, my breathing getting heavier as I start to move in rhythm against her – our – hands.

"I think I have it figured out. Tomorrow night I am collecting."

Her voice is deep and husky and I barely nod as she takes me to ecstasy.

Forty-Five: Mean Old Doc

I am nervous at breakfast when I see Shy Boy but he smiles at me, clear bright eyes twinkling like it didn't matter what happened on the couch and he loves me anyway and it was another eat them eggs and not puke start to the day.

"Just another day in paradise," the hedgehog sings.

He's right. I eat my eggs and they aren't slimy or runny they are just like ambrosia and I play footsies with Shy Boy under the table (not like Violet, foot to foot not foot to crotch) and Violet keeps saying "tonight, tonight," but I tune her out, I don't think about what kind of favor she could ask of me that I haven't done for her already.

Stuart counts the cameras and there aren't any new ones and inspects the spoons for any hidden transmitters and doesn't find any and even he has to admit that nothing horrible has happened yet. "Calm before the storm," the cow says, and Stuart nods his head thoughtfully.

We pick up our trays and head to morning session and we see exactly what the cow meant. Damn that precognitive bovine, there sits the mean old doc himself, clipboard and pen and paper in hand, sitting next to Andie. And to top it off Sam is there and not Kareem.

"Good morning," Andie starts, as if to say don't be scared, don't be worried, just because Doctor Martin is here I am still in charge and you are all still safe.

"You want me to make you a card?" Violet asks the doctor. "Course, there is a certain prerequisite to having a card. But it would be worth it, you would go out with a smile."

Sam keeps Violet from demonstrating just how happy she could make Doctor Martin. After we all get seated Andie continues.

"Okay, as you can see, Doctor Martin is here to observe again." She pauses. "He is here because I asked him, I think it is important for him to see how... well things are going for us."

"Screech!" Pet Shop shouts, flapping his arms. "Screech!"

"Well, that's a new one," says Doctor Martin.

"Herbert, please settle down. Tell us what is bothering you."

Pet Shop keeps flapping his arms and screeching.

"He's scared Doctor Martin is going to take away the hedgehog again," Stuart says. "He says last time he met with Doctor Martin he made him give up the hedgehog."

Andie looks at Doctor Martin. "Doctor?"

Doctor Martin looks a little embarrassed. "He wasn't talking. I merely told him that I would lock up his zoo if he didn't cooperate. Obviously you are encouraging the opposite, adding to his collection instead of eliminating his manifestations."

Andie gives him a "we will talk about this later" look. She turns to Pet Shop. "Herbert, I promise we will not do anything to your animals." He stops flapping his arms and quiets down.

"Gordon, I showed Doctor Martin your drawings on the cards. He was very impressed, weren't you, Doctor?"

Doctor Martin may not always get along with Andie, but even he knew to follow that lead. "Yes, Doctor MacPherson. They were very interesting. Very detailed. Very capable renditions. You are quite the artist, Gordon."

Shy Boy keeps his head down. There are beads of sweat on his brow; he is trembling a little. I think he is scared of Doctor Martin. But we all are, what is causing this reaction? What has changed – the drawings? Why does he care if Doctor Martin thinks he is a good artist?

Shy Boy just sits there and sweats and shakes. Andie reaches out, stroking his forearm, pulling him out of his isolation, back into the room with the rest of us. He lifts his head, meets her eyes; maybe for the first time, he looks into her eyes. I see his face lighten up as he is drawn into that angelic aura she projects. I see her own eyes widen at the recognition that Shy Boy is with us more now than he ever has been.

She releases him, and he hangs his head again. Doctor Martin, for all his being here to observe, appears to have missed this whole exchange. He taps his pen on the clipboard. "It doesn't look like Gordon wishes to share today," he says, and I try not to laugh and I can tell from the way Andie rolls her eyes that she can't believe the doctor is that thick-headed either. That he didn't see Shy Boy connect with Andie.

"I guess not," she says, but Shy Boy and I both know she is lying.

"Can I kiss you, Andie?" Violet asks. She must have seen the same thing. She doesn't ask like she wants to shock her or even Doctor Martin, she asks like it is the most important thing she could obtain, like it would be a gift from above, to taste the sweetness of her lips. She asks like she has seen Andie the protector once more keep us from the clutches of the evil one and she wants to breathe in the very essence of that soul that guards us.

The room is still, so sincere was the request, we all want to be Violet, we all want Andie to share this with her, to cross into our realm, to give us all through Violet's lips a taste of the infinite.

We all want that, that is, except the thickheaded idiot.

"We will not have indecent propositions, young lady," Doctor Martin says. "That is not permitted. There will be no kissing, no grabbing, no touching. And no talk of such. Understood?"

The atmosphere returns, we are once again in a room sitting in chairs with a couple doctors and even though one is an angel and one is a demon they are human again. Violet turns away and we never hear Andie's answer and we remain apart.

Forty-Six: Favors

Shy Boy is back to being shy after seeing Doctor Martin. He lets me hold his hand but he doesn't try anything else and I am worried that he doesn't like me anymore. Violet says don't worry, after tonight it will be okay, after tonight you will know how to make him happy and she keeps smiling and skipping around and I am not sure I want tonight, I think I want yesterday, but I can't stop it and soon it is lights out and I go to my room and put on my sleeping sweats and t-shirt and wait under the covers.

I lie in the darkness. I think about Shy Boy and Andie and Violet. How I love them all but in different ways. How they make me feel alive and good in different ways.

Before too long, Violet snuggles next to me. "Hey, sweetie," she says, "how's my favorite girl doing?"

Her hands roam over my body, circling my breasts, rubbing all over. "Strip," she whispers in my ear, "take everything off."

I strip completely, throwing my clothes to the side, and slide back under the sheet. I wait for her hands, her tongue, her love. I wait, breathing heavily, in anticipation.

I hear the door open.

I hear the footsteps cross the room.

I look up. He looms large in the darkness. I can't make out his face. "Shy Boy?" I ask.

"I'm not exactly shy," Sam says, the belt hitting the ground, his member sticking out near my face. "But you can call me anything you want, baby."

I want to scream. I want to run. I want to close my eyes and sleep and make it to the morning. My mouth opens, ready to release my terror into the dark, when she stops me.

Violet whispers, "It's okay, love, I asked him to be here. This is the favor you owe me, this is how I am collecting. I want you to do exactly what I tell you, what he tells you. What he wants. So you know how to do it with Shy Boy. So you can be happy."

She takes my hand and puts it on Sam's penis. "Come on, stroke it," she tells me, as Sam rocks his pelvis. He is large and stiff and I feel dirty and I don't want to touch him. I release him.

"Hey, you just got going, girl, don't stop now," Sam tells me.

"No, no more, I don't want to."

"You promised," Violet whispers. "This is good for you. For you and Shy Boy." She makes me pull the sheets down, exposing my body to Sam.

Sam smiles, "Okay, I guess if you are ready we can get right to it, we don't need any of that foreplay crap." He climbs into bed next to me, starts pawing at my breasts, kissing my neck, my ears, my face.

His hands are rough as they grab at me. I flinch when he squeezes my nipples.

"Sorry, baby, didn't mean to hurt you. It's just been a while and you have such a hot little body."

"Do it again," Violet tells him. "Squeeze them harder."

He does and I cry out a little and he laughs and says "crazy bitch."

I feel his hardness brushing against my leg. He reaches down, pushing a hand between my legs. Violet urges me to grind against his hand, to reach around and massage his butt, to enjoy the ride, to let myself go.

I try to pretend it is Violet inserting her fingers inside me but they are too big and too forceful and it is pain not pleasure they are inflicting. I struggle, I try to pull his arm up and his hand lands on my breast again and with Violet egging him on he thinks everything that is happening is what I want to happen and he is wrong and she is wrong and I am wrong.

"Okay, enough prep, huh? Let's get it on," he says, spreading my legs and rising above me and he is going to enter me. All of a sudden I smell cigars and aftershave and bacon burning and I cry out "No, don't do this Daddy, don't hurt me."

He stops. But just for a moment. "I'm not going to hurt you," Sam says. "I'm going to make you feel real good, I promise. Just like you asked me too."

And he moves against me and I feel him pressing into me and I shove him away with all my strength. He falls out of the bed and sits on the floor, stunned at my sudden resistance.

I stand over him, naked but armored in my resolve. "No!" I scream at him. "You can't do that, I don't care who you are or who I am, I say no! She can't give you my body and you can't take it. It's mine, nobody else's and you can't touch me unless I say so."

Sam sits there, his penis going limp as he listens to my tirade. "But you asked me – you told me to come tonight."

"No I didn't, Violet did, and she doesn't own me anymore. This isn't her body, she can't give it away anymore. Get out!" I throw his pants at him and he jumps into them and leaves.

I sit down on the bed — naked, alone, spent. I cry from the pain and the loneliness and the freedom I have found this night. I cry until I sleep, and there are no dreams, only an empty void that I know I must fill myself.

Forty-Seven: All Grown Up

Breakfast is somber. I sit there, picking at my eggs, not really eating anything. Shy Boy is still acting withdrawn; Pet Shop is having a quiet conversation with the cow and the hedgehog. The third time I don't answer him Stuart figures out that I don't feel like talking.

I follow them to morning session. Andie is waiting for us. With Sam. I don't look at him and he doesn't look at me. At least Doctor Martin isn't there.

"Good morning, everyone. Who wants to start?" Why is she always so cheerful, so completely Andie, I wonder. How can each day start like last night didn't happen? That there wasn't a strange man invited into your bed by your best friend? That your best friend didn't leave you forever. Again.

The silence hangs and Violet isn't here to break it up and Andie must know something is wrong, can't she tell?

"Strangers in the night," says the hedgehog and I give Pet Shop my stare that says if looks could kill you would be pushing up daisies and he gives me a what, don't blame the messenger shrug as if he didn't know the hedgehog was going to talk. How the hell did that thing ever keep any of our plans secret?

"That is an interesting point," Andie says, and I realize she knew something was up all along she just wanted us to say it first. "There were a few disturbances last night, from what I have heard. Anybody care to discuss those?"

Sam keeps not looking at me and I wonder if I should rat on him but it was really Violet not Sam so I look at Shy Boy instead and I jump in my seat because he saw me looking at Sam and has the angriest expression on his face I have ever seen. He quickly looks down and hides his face and Andie takes my movement as an opening and asks, "What happened last night, Daphne?"

She sees Shy Boy hiding his face and I am blushing and I don't know what to tell her. "Did Gordon visit you? I know what happened on the couch when you were watching TV. Daphne, if Gordon was in your room last night you must tell me. Please, for both of you, tell me what happened. I promise neither of you will get in trouble, but you have to tell me what happened."

Those eyes, those soul-capturing eyes, pull me in and I want to tell her everything about how I was strong and kept my body my own but I don't know how to. And I don't want to get Sam in trouble, even if he called me a crazy bitch. And I especially don't want Shy Boy to think I did it with Sam, when I wouldn't let him even touch my breast.

"It wasn't Shy Boy," I say, and I see Sam swaying in the background, knowing I hold his job in my hands, knowing a few words and he is done for. "It was Violet." And Sam looks relieved but Shy Boy doesn't, Shy Boy doesn't believe this lie I tell, and he is looking at Sam and looking at me and I silently pray he isn't thinking what I know he is thinking.

"Violet came to me last night," I tell Andie, looking at her lips, the curl of hair over her ears, the rims of her glasses. Anywhere but in the eyes. I cast my own gaze down, feigning shyness and embarrassment, trying to convince her it is the words and the deeds that are causing my difficulties, not the fact that I am lying to the herald of Eden. "She came to me, and we took off our clothes, and she wanted, well she wanted us to do things. To touch. To kiss. To make love."

"Violet came to me and she demanded these things. She wanted to own me, to possess me, to control me. She wanted everything I had." I look up at Andie. These words were truthful, I could face her for these. "And I decided that it was my body, no one else's. That it was my choice who could touch me and where they could touch me and when they could touch me. I wasn't going to let her do that to me anymore." I looked down again, prepared for my final lie. "So I cast her out of my bed, and she wasn't happy and we yelled at each other until she left. That was what all the commotion was about." More truth now, to seal my story, to close the lie. "So Violet's gone now. She knows I don't need her. She isn't coming back. I hope she finds her way to Glen and Theodore, she'd be happier with them anyway."

Andie hugs me and tells me she is so proud of me for making the right choices. That I was right, that it was my body, that I didn't need Violet, I was a grown woman and could take care of myself. And I cry on her shoulder, all grown up and bawling like a baby. "I'm going to miss Violet," I sob, "she was my best friend. My bestest friend since Melissa."

"I know, I know she was," Andie says, stroking my hair, holding me tight, lending me her strength. Andie holds me and I let her, it isn't the same as Violet but in some ways it is better. Cleaner. More caring. Less needing.

Through my tears I see Sam thanking his gods in silent prayer. I look over at Shy Boy and he isn't crying and he isn't happy and he doesn't seem shy in the least.

Forty-Eight: Kareem And Shy Boy

We are sitting at lunch. It is still pretty quiet. Shy Boy is at least looking at me again and when I smile at him he gives me a little one back. Maybe he was listening at session. He knows Violet is gone, so hopefully he bought the whole story.

Pet Shop is going around to all the tables and getting leftover vegetables. He is worried that the screech owl isn't getting a balanced diet. Too much toast, I suppose, isn't good for owls. I offer him my carrots and a couple spoonfuls of applesauce.

"Violet left on purpose, right? She wasn't abducted, was she?"

"No, Stuart, no one took her. I told you, she decided she wasn't needed anymore. She left, that's all there was to it."

"Good. Not good that she's gone, good that there wasn't a government strike force picking us off one by one. Because that is how they would do it. We'd disappear one by one until nobody was left and they would take it all over. One by one, that's how it works."

"No abduction. No kidnapping. She just left."

Shy Boy moves his chair closer to me. He takes my hand, raises it to his lips, and gives a soft prince charming pleased to meet the princess kiss on it. I ignore Stuart's continuing rant about government strike forces taking us out one by one and look at Shy Boy and I get goose bumps.

"Shy Boy, what are –" I start but he puts a finger to my lips and says "shhhh" and that is the loudest sound I have ever heard him utter and he brushes the hair out of my eyes and leans in and kisses me on the forehead and then on the cheek and then on the lips and it is passionate but not devouring and I am still me and it doesn't consume me and it is the best kiss I have ever had.

I hear the throat clearing and I pull back from Shy Boy's kiss and Kareem is standing there, shaking his head. "Now, now, boys and girls," he says, sternly but not so much that we think we are actually in trouble. "We can't be necking in the lunch room.

Too many health code violations with all that bodily fluid swapping."

Stuart giggles and I blush and Shy Boy just gives a wolfish grin like he gets caught making out all the time. "Sorry, Kareem," I tell him but he knows I'm not and I know he doesn't really care, that he is glad we are finding happiness.

"You two just be careful, okay? Don't let things get out of hand. Or out of control. Understand, Gordon? Don't let little Gordon do your thinking, capiche?"

Shy Boy keeps smiling but Kareem stares him down until finally he nods his head. "Good," Kareem says. "And you, young lady, don't be getting Gordon too riled up."

"Yes sir, Mister Kareem, I'll be good."

"Don't sass me, Daphne," he says, shaking his finger at me. We both laugh.

I watch him walk away and I wonder what would have happened had Violet invited Kareem instead of Sam. It would have been different, that's for sure. But he wouldn't be Kareem if that was something he would have agreed to, that's why she had to settle for Sam.

I look around and only see Sam standing guard over us and I know he isn't going to bust me in the near future so I lean back over to Shy Boy and plant a real juicy one on him. I whisper in his ear, "I can't wait for Wheel of Fortune" and he gets a great big smile on his face and kisses me again.

Forty-Nine: The Mystery Of Melissa

"Daphne, tell me about Melissa."

It is afternoon session and I stare at Andie and wonder how in the hell she knows about Melissa? "Who?" I play dumb, hoping this is all a mistake.

She brings soft brown orbs of entrapment into play, peering through the depths of my heart and soul. "This morning, you mentioned her. That she was your best friend before Violet."

I must have said it when I was grieving over losing Violet. That's not fair, using information obtained under false pretenses. Except I know there was nothing false about how she cared for me, about how she held me. Nothing false except the story I had told her.

"She was," I admit. I can't keep it from her. I can't keep the shields in place; I can't bury it behind lies or walls of silence. "She was my best friend when I was a little girl. She was the only one I could talk to. The only one who would listen. Who could understand."

Andie takes my hand, giving me comfort, urging me on. Compelling me through spirit just when I had achieved control over body.

I take a deep breath and force it out. "Whenever Dad… visited me, she would be there for me. Whenever Mom turned up the TV so she couldn't hear me, Melissa would listen to my cries. She promised that everything would be okay, that one day Dad would turn back into Daddy and Mom would be Mommy and I could play dress up instead of dress off. That sitting on Dad's lap would be safe. That I could be a little girl again."

"What happened to her?" Andie asks.

"The night that Mom walked in on Dad's visit – no, I've called them visits too often, they were anything but visits." I turn embarrassment to anger. Choose bluntness over euphemisms. "The night that Mom walked in on Dad raping me. Not visiting, raping. That night when Dad went running out of the room after her and I heard Mom yelling at him and then I heard nothing, Melissa told me it was all going to be better now. That everything would be how it was supposed to be in the morning. That Mom would fix Dad and we would be a family and live happily ever after."

Tears brim in Andie's eyes as I pour my life into her open hands. "She lied."

"Daphne," Andie started, wanting to hold me, to heal me. But I held back, needing to finish. There wasn't much more to tell, it would be better to get it over with.

"So Melissa talked to me through the night, promising me the world and I believed in it more than Santa Claus, more than the sun rising in the east. We talked and held onto each other and I didn't even go to sleep because I was worried that I would miss the change and sleep through it and if I wasn't awake then maybe it would skip right back to normal. Bad normal, not good normal. When morning finally came I went downstairs and sat down at the kitchen table and all that changed was extra strawberries and home made waffles and I realized that Melissa was as powerless against him as I was. I never talked to her again."

I am ready now, and let her hold me. She is crying more than I am and it is strange how I have never let any of the others know about Melissa and now it doesn't even matter to me. Not when fireplaces and romance novels and maple syrup and staying up until three a.m. drinking wine is holding me in her arms.

Shy Boy gets up out of his chair and joins our hug and then Pet Shop does too and Stuart is there too and I feel a little tiny piece of Melissa saying she was sorry she wanted to help me but Daddy was just too big and strong and then my tears come out in torrents.

"I forgive you, Melissa," I tell her and I know somewhere, maybe with Glen and Theodore and Violet, she is happy for the first time since I drove her away.

Sam doesn't join our group, he just stands and watches but I can tell he wanted to. Whether out of genuine sympathy or to cop a feel, I don't know.

Fifty: Clean Wheel Of Fortune Is Boring

It just isn't the same playing Wheel of Fortune without Violet. I look at the puzzle and at least three profane possibilities occur to me but I know, even if I shout them out, it won't be Violet, it won't be funny, so I keep my dirty words to myself.

Shy Boy and I are snuggled on the couch. He tries to pull the blanket up but I don't let him. "I'm not quite ready for that, Shy Boy," I say, but I give him a kiss and brush his hair back with my hand, and he smiles and accepts the boundary lines as I have drawn them.

Sam walks over. "Hey, Daphne, can I see you for a second?" he asks. I get off of the couch and walk over to the corner. I feel Shy Boy's eyes following us the whole time.

"What do you want?"

"I just wanted to thank you, for, you know, covering for me this morning. Not that I did anything wrong, I was invited –"

"By Violet, not me," I tell him.

"Sure, sure, but it's not like I forced my way in. Violet told me you wanted to do it with me, wanted a man to teach you stuff, so you could make your boyfriend there happy."

"Yeah, I guess I could see her saying that."

"So, what I'm saying is, I got no hard feelings over last night."

"What do you mean?"

Sam leers at me. "If you still, you know, need me to show you the ropes, I could come by tonight."

I stand there, flushing red from anger or embarrassment or both. He sees my reaction to his words and starts backing away.

"Now, girly, don't get upset, I was just offering, that's all."

"Get out of here before I take that dick you are thinking with and shove it down your throat."

Sam turns and quickly exits the room. I go back to the couch and try to calm down. I can't believe he thought that I wanted to do anything with him, how desperate can he be? Or how desperate does he think I am? I mean, geez, I threw his pants at him and kicked him out last night!

Shy Boy touches my arm to get my attention and I have to catch myself to keep from slapping him. "Oh, Shy Boy, I'm sorry, I didn't mean to scare you," I tell him.

His eyes tighten and he looks at the door that Sam left through and gets that angry look on his face again. "It's nothing, Shy Boy, Sam didn't do anything; I can handle him."

I'm not certain he believes me — maybe I am lying so much now that they are easier to notice. I stroke his arm a little and rub his chest a little and kiss him a little more than a little until we hear "lights out in five minutes."

Fifty-One: Dream A Little Dream

It is a slumber party and I am in pajamas but it's okay I like them. They are soft and snuggly and besides Melissa and Andie and Violet are all wearing pajamas too. Daddy pokes his head in and says, "Good night girls, don't stay up too late," and I say, "Aw, Daddy, we won't" and he smiles and all the girls giggle and he shuts the door. Violet says Daddy seems nice and Melissa looks at me and I ignore her and say, "Yes, he is very nice." Andie just listens to us talk.

We sit in a circle and braid each other's hair. I braid Andie's and Andie braids Melissa's and Melissa braids Violet's and Violet braids mine. They are the bestest friends in the whole wide world.

"I want to stay up all night," I tell them.

Melissa looks at me. "Is it safer to stay up or sleep?" she asks.

"What do you mean?" Andie asks.

Violet pulls my hair back, leaning over from behind, looking at my upside down face. "I say we stay up. I have all kinds of games we can play."

Andie says, "I don't like those kinds of games. I think we should just play normal stuff. We can talk about boys and play with dolls and put on makeup."

Melissa starts to cry. "I want to go to sleep. If we go to sleep and don't wake up until morning then we are safe."

"You're just a baby," Violet tells her. "If you can't play big girl games then you just go ahead and go to bed. Alone."

"Melissa, wait," I call but she is gone.

Violet looks at me, looks at Andie. "What's it going to be, Daphne? You want someone to make you feel good, to liberate you? You want someone to let you enjoy what is going to happen to you anyway? May as well sit back and enjoy the ride, I always say."

She isn't a little girl and she isn't wearing pajamas and her lust emanates from her and I feel the hunger, the ache, and the emptiness inside me, longing to be filled by her passion. To wash it away in a frenzy of satiation and fulfillment.

I reach toward her, wanting to cling and thrust and grind against her body. I put my hand out, but Andie reaches me first. She places her hand onto my shoulder, blocking my way. "Daphne, you've been here already," she says. "You've escaped from this illusion before. Remember, this is your body, your soul, she can't make either whole."

And I grow up into a woman and I am in sweats and a t-shirt and Andie is in a skirt and a sweater and she is beyond lust and beyond safety. I know I want her in the way I wanted Violet. I know I need her protection the way Melissa tried to shield me from harm. I know she is all I have ever sought after and I know she will never be mine the way I want but I look over her shoulder and Violet sees my choice and then she is gone. Gone like Melissa.

Before she can stop me I lean up and in for one quick taste and Violet was right, Andie is sweet, sweet as anything I have ever taken in, and I wake up and I am smiling and there are birds singing and I want to squirm further under the covers and hold onto this feeling as long as I can before it fades away and reality settles into its daily rendition that is anything but what my dreams have presented. When they aren't nightmares, that is. Reality matches the nightmares all too often.

Fifty-Two: Doctor Martin's Fascination

I walk into morning session still carrying a tinge of last night's dream with me. Just enough to carry me right past the venomous figure of Doctor Martin, who we are ever so privileged to have among us once more.

"Good morning," Andie greets us and I give her a big smile and she notices I'm in a good mood, she has to, how can she not when every fiber of my being is reaching out and forging the bond between us, making it stronger every time our eyes meet, our hands clasp, our lips – no, that was just a dream, I know it was just a dream. But still, what a dream it was.

"Superfreak," says the hedgehog.

Stuart giggles.

"I wanted to spend a little more time with you today," Doctor Martin says. "I thought we could do a little project together."

Stuart perked up. "Project? What type of project – we won't be part of illegal government experiments funded by gasoline taxes, I tell you we won't participate in such a scheme!"

"Nothing like that. I just want to get some pictures to put on the walls in the cafeteria. I thought we could all walk down to the art room and draw some nice pictures to brighten the place up."

"Sounds better than talking to you," I say. Doctor Martin seems a little taken aback, but I wasn't being rude. Just honest. And it's not like he doesn't know we don't like talking to him.

We go to the art room and Andie hands out paper and markers to everyone. "Draw whatever is on your minds," Doctor Martin instructs. "Your feelings, your dreams. What you like doing. What you wish you could do. Anything that is on your mind. Don't worry, if you don't want everyone else to see we won't hang it up, it's up to you."

"Can we draw more than one?" Pet Shop asks. "I don't think I can fit the hedgehog and the cow on the same sheet."

"That's fine, Herbert. You can draw as many as you want."

Pet Shop smiles and proceeds with his pictures. I look at my blank piece of paper. It's just like the cards, trying to decide what to pull from nothing and make something, except this time it is about me, not about the dead people.

Stuart is placing a bunch of zeroes and ones on his paper. I think it is secret code. Probably a real code that will bring the real government down on him to find out how he cracked it.

Shy Boy is hiding his paper, crouched over it so no one can see it. He is drawing rapidly, his hand racing back and forth. Doctor Martin tries to peek at it and Shy Boy turns his chair and keeps it out of the doctor's view.

Pet Shop is on his third page and I haven't started my first. I look to see what he has drawn and smile. They are perfect for him. He has three almost identical pages, each a pastoral scene with a big empty space where whatever invisible animal he is drawing must be.

I take a marker and start sketching. I remember the feeling I awoke with, the dream set in past but looking toward the future, and the lines start falling in place. My abilities as an artist fall far short of the vision in my mind, but I do my best. I draw my feelings, my dreams, what I want, just as Doctor Martin asked for. I draw brown eyes and pearl white skin and a curl of hair over her ear. I draw black-rimmed glasses that are a trifle too low on her nose. I draw a sweater and stick a couple leaves on it. I draw full lips with a touch of honey rolling off of them. I draw my dream, I draw my Andie.

I feel her looking over my shoulder. She must recognize it, I hope she recognizes it, oh, please recognize it, Andie. She gives my shoulder a little squeeze and I blush and I'm so glad I didn't butcher it so badly that she couldn't tell who it was.

"Very nice, Daphne," Doctor Martin says, and I am embarrassed, I didn't draw it for him but I don't care because Andie liked it. I mumble thanks and start scribbling on another sheet of paper until he moves on.

He picks up Pet Shop's papers and makes nice comments about each of them and I wonder just what the bad doctor is up to. Out of the corner of my eye I see Shy Boy hide a drawing under his shirt.

When Doctor Martin gets to Shy Boy he picks up the drawing that Shy Boy didn't stash away and looks at it without saying a word. He shows it to Andie who says, "That's very nice, Gordon," but I see disappointment in her eyes. Shy Boy must have caught it too because he hangs his head and stares straight down.

I catch a glimpse of the drawing in Doctor Martin's hands and it is just a bunch of stick people, nothing special, even worse than the one he drew when Stuart was making aerial surveillance maps.

When we are walking back from session I grab Shy Boy's hand and we let the others go on ahead. "Shy Boy, I saw you hide the other picture. What was it? Why didn't you want Doctor Martin to see it?"

He stands there, holding my hand, looking me straight in the eye, not blinking, trying to connect but not having the words. I smile and give him a little kiss and tell him, "It's okay, if you don't want to show me, you don't have to. You respected my boundaries, you can have yours too."

I start to walk away and he pulls me back. He slowly reaches under his shirt and pulls out the picture. He turns it over so I can see it.

"Shy Boy, it's…" I don't know what to say. It's a drawing of me! But it's not really me, it's someone beautiful. Naked, but beautiful. Not me, but it is me, and this is how he sees me? Naked, but not dirty. I can't believe he thinks I look like this. Naked, but strong, not exposed, not vulnerable, not anything like I really am. This isn't what I see when I look in the mirror. Not even close. How can he see me like this? How can anyone look at the wreck that I am and come away with this picture?

"It's wonderful," I finally tell him. I hug him tight and kiss him hard on the lips and tell him he is too good to be true and thank him for sharing it with me and not Doctor Martin. I reluctantly return the picture to him but I know I will never forget not just the picture but what it felt like to realize that someone looked at me and envisioned that drawing.

Fifty-Three: Remembering The Dead

We walk into afternoon session and Kareem is sitting there and I see the package he is carrying and I point it out to Stuart.

Stuart – Stuart, mind you! – runs up to Kareem and hugs him. "Thank you for your dedication to this solemn task," he says. "The legacy left behind will be restored. The nameless named, the forgotten remembered, the lost found. I salute you."

"Well, I guess you have figured out what Kareem brought us," Andie says. "Yes, the engraver called, said the plaque was done, and Kareem volunteered to pick it up on his lunch hour."

"A scholar and a gentleman," the cow moos.

"Thanks for picking it up, Kareem," I tell him. "This means a lot to me – to all of us."

"No problem, it was a nice day for a drive."

"And a nice day for putting up a plaque," Andie adds. "Sam is already out at the cemetery with the setting stone, let's not keep him waiting any longer."

So off we go. I keep trying to catch Shy Boy's hand but he is back to being shy. He glances at me occasionally and it seems that he is checking to make sure I am okay but for some reason he is playing it like he is the old Shy Boy.

"We're off to see the wizard," says the hedgehog, and again he has captured our mood succinctly. Stuart is carrying the plaque high over his head, leading the triumphant procession to the cemetery.

I watch Andie and Kareem walking side by side, talking so easily, so naturally, that I wonder if they are more than co-workers. The flare of jealousy doesn't become such a wonderful occasion and I quickly douse it. Andie is just so empathic and Kareem so nice but always a friend that the ridiculousness of the combination eliminates any further consideration of hidden relations between the two.

We arrive and see Sam has been busy. He has already prepped the site, having mowed a little clearing in the front center area of the cemetery, just inside the broken gate. A new block of stone sitting there, its bright white surface a sharp contrast to the weathered grays of the surrounding tombstones.

"All set, Andie," Sam tells her. "I have the holes drilled already, I can bolt it on whenever you want."

"Great job, Sam." She takes the plaque from Stuart and passes it to Sam, who installs it on the stone block. It doesn't take long; minutes later he steps back so we can all get a good look at our work.

"It's perfect," Andie says, and I nod my head in agreement. It is simple, but profound to those of us who can relate to it – relate to those whom it honors.

"Read it to us, Andie, please," Pet Shop asks.

"IN MEMORIAL OF THE PEOPLE OF KANAPOLIS SANITARIUM. FOR THOSE BURIED HERE, MAY THEY NEVER BE FORGOTTEN, MAY THEIR NAMES BE KNOWN. WE DEDICATE THIS TO SOME, SO THAT ALL MAY BE HONORED."

Underneath the words are the individual plates made from our cards. I trace the names, the engraved drawings giving each of them not only their name but uniqueness as well. I marvel again at the intricacies of Shy Boy's plates. Detailed or not, they are all respectful of those who were here before us. People just like me: lost, confused, abandoned. But deserving more. Deserving to be held, to be comforted. To be known.

Stuart kneels beside the tombstone with three seven dash four three three on it. He kisses it as Violet did in the past. He rests his forehead against the stone and starts shaking, tears rolling down his cheek. Violent sobs rack his body.

Andie kneels beside him and he throws himself into her arms and she strokes his head and rocks him back and forth. "It's all right, Stuart. No one will forget them now. No one will be a number anymore."

He looks up into her eyes. He is crying and smiling simultaneously. "I know," he says. "I'm so happy for them. But I'm sad. I'm so sad."

"Why, Stuart? This is a celebration, why are you unhappy?"

Stuart reaches for her hand, holds it tightly. I feel him clasping her hand. I feel his sorrow, and know why it is there. He looks at her. I look at her. My eyes are filled with Stuart's tears. I want to cry out, to tell him I still need him, but he won't listen. I hear him say the words. I hear him tell Andie goodbye.

Andie stares into my tear-brimmed eyes. She doesn't understand. Not at first. Slowly I see the comprehension come, as she realizes who it is she is now looking at. I feel the blood rush out of my face, I feel the gaping emptiness inside me, I feel the world spinning me into the heart of the sun and then I give in and collapse into her arms.

Fifty-Four: Two Lights

I sink through the endless void, the deep stillness of eternal darkness that I have traversed before. The hollowness within my corporeal shell mirrors that which surrounds me. Where once lived many now only one remains. The protector from harm, the guardian of change, the caretaker of emotions, the shield against assimilation – all have left, all have abandoned me.

I reach inside and I find resistance. Strength. Self-confidence. I reach deeper and find love. Acceptance. Understanding. I scrutinize all that I have become, that their passing has transformed me, galvanized what were disparate fragments of being into a whole. Fragile yet durable as a sapling is. Able to survive the gale as it bends while the stubborn oak cracks in its inflexibility.

I cast my vision across the cosmos and it is only through my eyes that I see. I sing hosannas to the outer reaches of infinity and my ears alone hear the echoes. I bare my body to the universe and feel solar flares, asteroids, galaxies caress my skin and the ecstasy is solely mine.

I embrace all that I am as I release all that I was. Glen, Theodore, Violet, Stuart. Even Melissa. They are part of me and always will be, but it is Daphne who will command the vessel that carries us all.

Two beacons appear. I am drawn to them, twin points of light set against the ocean of black. They call to me, and I am entire enough to answer. I swim rapidly to them, eager to escape from this solitary confinement. I reach for them, I beseech them, to pull me free, to take me home.

"Daphne," the sirens sing in unison. "Come back to us."

"Help me," I plead, "deliver me from this prison I have built."

The lights mutate as I approach. The one on the left slowly changes into Shy Boy – no, Gordon, he is too complete, too alive, to be Shy Boy anymore. The one on the right transforms into Andie.   They both reach out to me, to pull me to safety, to bring me out of the depths I have fallen to.   I try to grasp both their hands but they are too far apart, I cannot stretch enough to span the distance between them. I start drifting away.

"Daphne, please, take my hand," Gordon says. He is at once the never been kissed and first dance and prom and maidenhead taking white picket fence and two and a half kids everything that a man could be.

"Daphne, let me save you," Andie says. She is sweaters and pajamas and leaves and clinging and sweet gentle hands and softness and purring and everything that a woman could be.

Their eyes are full of love and promises and happily ever after and I can't decide and I drift away as they continue to offer all that I ever wanted. I look above as the figures become shining stars and the points of light and then even those fade. Then there is nothing.

Fifty-Five: Gordon

I wake and I am in my bed and somebody has dressed me in pajamas again. I wonder who stripped my clothes off, who saw me naked before clothing me in my sleepwear. It doesn't really matter. Whatever they saw would pale in contrast to the nakedness of my soul. Unless it was Sam, whose putting me to bed would perhaps not solely consist of a change of clothes. I wonder if I could even tell if I had been violated while I was out of it. Surely I would have experienced nightmares of my past abuses, rather than the celestial wanderings and visions I recall from last night.

I shake off thoughts of Sam and any potential assaults. He may be crude and obnoxious but if he was prone to rape he would never have left my room the night Violet had invited him in. I get out of bed and change out of the pajamas and into a t-shirt and jeans. The t-shirt is insufficient; I add a sweatshirt over it. It is warmer but there is still a coldness inside that no layering of garments will defrost.

Breakfast. I walk in to the cafeteria and Pet Shop and Gordon are there. Even awake, his manifestation sustains, I no longer see him as Shy Boy. He lifts his head in greeting as I sit, his eyes crystal, his lips forming the bridge to eternity that I was unable to cross last night. As empty as I am now, doubtless he has been filled equally, and he is so present that I can do nothing else but smile as I bask in his glow.

"Hey, you," I say, not sure how he would react if I called him Gordon. Not sure if I want to make it that apparent that I view him differently.

"Yea, though we walk in the shadow of the valley," offers the hedgehog. Quite a solemn choice for the normally sarcastic fur ball.

"Good morning, Pet Shop. You too, hedgehog,"

I eat a couple pieces of toast. While Gordon has lifted my spirits I am still so uncertain. He is overpowering next to me, but

I cannot fool myself into thinking that I will not be as swept away in another direction the moment Andie is near.

It is quiet, eating breakfast with Gordon and Pet Shop. All the usual suspects, with the exception of the hedgehog, are absent. No tangential observations from the paranoid set, no sexual innuendoes or trouser attacks, just a couple people eating food. What used to take forty-five minutes is over in ten.

We sit there at the table, Pet Shop playing with the remains of his breakfast, and Gordon and I staring at each other. Finally I give in to half of my heart. I tell Pet Shop we will meet him at morning session, take Gordon's hand and lead him back to my room.

I sit down on the bed, motion for him to sit beside me. He takes my hands in his, lifts them to his lips, and brushes tender kisses against them. I close my eyes, drinking in the caresses, the touches of his lips as he travels from hand to forearm to shoulder. He nuzzles my neck, his hot breath as he exhales soaks through the frost that had filled me since I awoke, thawing the blocks of ice surrounding my heart. Half of it, anyway.

Half of it. I know it is only half. That he is offering all and I am not prepared to reciprocate. Even though in his arms I am ready to make love, to lose myself in passion and to thrust in rhythm with eager anticipation, I cannot continue. I open my eyes, capture his hands before they can rove across my chest, pull back from his embrace. I meet his gaze, see everything that could exist alive in those sparkling orbs, and turn it away.

His arms drop, his shoulders slump, tears roll down his cheeks. His incomprehension resonates through every movement his body makes.

"I'm sorry. I want this as much as you do, believe me I am aching inside. I just – I can't – I –" Tears fall from my own eyes as I struggle to find the words to explain what I don't fully understand myself.

He lifts my head up, smiles gently. He brushes my hair back, leans in, and kisses me. Not a "let's make love" kiss, not a hello or goodbye kiss, but a "hey, let's just kiss and it will be all better next time" kiss. An "I understand, even if you don't" kiss. Almost a kiss to claim all of me.

"I love you, I really do," I tell him. "I love you, Gordon." He is Gordon now; he will always be Gordon.

His eyes go wide as he hears his name. I take advantage of his surprise to lean in and return the kiss. A "thank you, I love you, even if I am an idiot" kiss.

Fifty-Six: Anyone Else In There?

I hold hands with Gordon all the way into morning session. I hold onto him until we sit down and I look over and Andie is sitting there with her black-rimmed glasses and divine presence and curl of hair over her ear and Gordon's hand just slips out of my grasp. Slips away and I can hardly remember what it was like to hold it.

"Good morning," Andie says, and I look at her pearl white skin and I notice a freckle on the side of her nose I have never seen before and I wonder how I ever could have missed something as beautiful as that. "How are you feeling this morning, Daphne?"

I smile and I want to hide and I try to reach Gordon thinking maybe that could anchor me but he doesn't notice, his hands are on his lap and I bite my lower lip and hope she asks someone else.

Andie reaches out and the bridge is there again, a span I must choose to cross and I think it is only fair, I shared with Gordon earlier, so I shift my hand from moving toward Gordon to intercepting her own and I allow her to pull me close. Closer than she expected I think because she gives a little start as my face is next to hers and I breathe in her perfume and I am shaking.

"Daphne?" she asks, not knowing who it is, so I give her a timid half-nod and a nervous smile. Have I changed so much that she no longer recognizes me?

"Andie," I whisper. "Andie, I don't know what's left of me. I've lost so much. Everyone's gone, everyone but you and Gordon."

"Oh sweet dear, you haven't lost, you've gained." She strokes my hair in mirror to Gordon's own acts of comfort. "They aren't gone, they are a part of you. You have their essence inside; they will always be there to help you. But you are strong enough now that you don't need them to live your life. To act on your behalf."

Her words recall many of my own reflections from my dream last night. I lift my head to look at her radiance, her smile, her teary eyes, burn through the other half of my frozen heart. I reach an arm around the back of her head and pull her toward me.

Our lips meet. I taste the moon, luminescent tendrils of joy run like a river through my veins. Briefly it seems she returns the kiss, but then she tries to pull away. I hold one hand firmly behind her head, pressing my lips on hers, the other hand around her waist, trying to keep her from escaping, wishing to turn this moment from one second to a century, no, that would not be enough, wishing to stop time itself with our lips joined.

She stands up, breaking my grip on head and waist. She is blushing and furious and Gordon is staring at me and Kareem is running over to get between us. I look at her; I look at someone I love. I look at someone I just forced myself on. Changing love to anger, possibly fear. I hang my head in shame.

Kareem puts a hand on my shoulder. "Come on, Daphne."

I lift my head. Andie is avoiding my eyes, trying to calm down. "Andie," I say. "I'm sorry. That was against everything you taught me. I didn't have the right to... invade your space. To kiss you without permission. I just... I love you, Andie. I know that doesn't make it right. But I do. So I'm sorry. Oh God, I'm sorry. I don't want to be like *him*, God help me I don't."

She stands there, still not looking at me. I take Kareem's arm. "Okay, Kareem, I'm ready."

We're at the door when she calls out to stop. She walks up, the angel of mercy, the soul of redemption, half of my heart. She comes up, and as soon as she meets my eyes I know that Armageddon is at least another day away, that there is still hope and dreams and prayers and love left in the world. She gives a small half-smile. No hug, but the half-smile was far more than I deserved.

"You've been through a lot the last few weeks, Daphne. I know it has been hard on you, but please know that I am very proud of you. Now get some rest and we will talk some more this afternoon, okay?" I blink the tears away and shake my head in agreement.

"And no more uninvited kisses." But she says it with a smile, a full one this time, and not a hell will freeze over before we ever touch again look. On the way back to my room I wonder if there will ever be invited kisses.

Fifty-Seven: Rest And Reflections

Kareem takes me to my room, suggests I take a nap, and I say okay but as soon as he leaves I am out the door. I know Andie said to get some rest but I do not want to face these emotions in my sleep. I need to address these conflicts, these thoughts, these desires in waking mode, to allow conscious decision on my life. To accept them. To accept me.

My feet follow natural, familiar paths as I try to sort out my feelings for Andie versus my feelings for Gordon. I look up and am not overly surprised to see the broken down fence and the numbered tombstones of the cemetery. The bright white stone with its memorial plaque shines in stark contrast to the rest, a beacon of promises, of acknowledgement, against the stale backdrop of death and anonymity.

I read the metal plates affixed to the plaque. Norman Jameson, Mary Franklin, Peter, Felicia, Samantha, Felix Potato. So many people who lived here, seeking help, looking to find meaning in a world that had none for them. Did they love each other? I wonder. Did they have their Andie to hold them and care about them and make it all seem better even when it wasn't? Did they have an anchor to hold them fast against the chaos surrounding them? Were they blessed, too?

"Screech!" calls Pet Shop's friend. I search for him among the branches of the big tree. There he is, watching me watching the past, doubtless waiting to see if I have brought more toast. Having no concern over what happened decades ago. Or what might happen decades from now. He cares for today. He lives in the moment. And I think that maybe I should do the same.

I have been reliving my past for years. I have sacrificed my present in constant suffering over what was done to me. Over the abuse by my dad, over the acceptance of it by my mom. Over things which I had no control over. No ability to change, to escape, to survive.

I have no precognitive talent to espy the proper course I should pursue. I have no indication that I could ever truly live a normal life, with Gordon or with Andie. That either of them would attempt it with me. But I refuse to let the potential nightmares of the future paralyze my present as I have let those of the past do. Regardless of who will return my love, of who I love the most, I owe it to myself to give out that love. To live in the real world — to be a part of that great mass of humanity which I have shunned for so long.

"Carpe Diem!" I shout to the screech owl.

.

Fifty-Eight: Prognosis Good

The walk helped. I see two paths before me, to match the halves of my heart. That is more than I saw before, when all that existed was a mirror showing me the past that controlled my life. A mirror that reflected the multiple facets of my self-image. Those facets have merged, I am whole now, and though I will always miss them they will always be part of me.

I walk confidently into the afternoon session, eager to share with Andie my internal reasoning. To show her how she has assisted in my journey from the past to the present. To ask her to continue on that journey on into the future.

Gordon is there already, as is Pet Shop, Andie and regrettably Doctor Martin. Kareem is also standing by, keeping a watchful eye on me. I give him a thumbs-up, letting him know I am not going to attack anyone's lips.

"Daphne," Doctor Martin begins, and I have a slight panic attack as I discover he is not only here to observe this time, "I'm glad you felt up to joining us this afternoon. Did you find your rest relaxing?"

Andie told him about the kiss. I can tell, the way he looks at me, checking my reaction, seeing if it is really me pulling the strings. Hunting for Violet, I suppose.

"It was fine," I say, not giving in to the desire to launch myself across the room and knock him off of his chair. Not wanting to give him the satisfaction of thinking he can affect me.

"Good. Doctor MacPherson and I have been discussing your situation. She believes that you have been improving lately. That you are controlling your actions more consistently. More responsibly. More..." He pauses. "...appropriately."

She didn't tell him after all, I realize. Kareem gives me a wink. He and Andie must have decided to keep Doctor Martin in the dark about this morning. She must have believed me when I said I was sorry, that I knew it was wrong. Everything I figured out at the cemetery this morning, she must have already known.

"I agree with Doctor MacPherson. You are responding very well to her treatment. What we would like to do is take the next step. This weekend, we are going to have you stay in another facility. A house in town, fully staffed but with more exposure to regular activities. To more people. Just for the weekend, to see how you like it."

The outside world. The real world. I don't know what to think of what he is telling me. Away from here? Away from Gordon and Andie? I look at Andie, seeking reassurance, verification that this is her plan too, and not simply an avenue of Doctor Martin's to separate me from those I love.

"Daphne," Andie says, clasping my hands in hers. "This is a good thing. Trust Doctor Martin and me. If we didn't think you were ready to try this we wouldn't be doing this. There will be people there to help you if you get scared or confused. It will almost be like living here, you will just meet some new people. You'll have a little more freedom in your schedule, to do the things you feel like doing. To try some new things, like helping cook dinner or washing your clothes."

"Will you be there?" I ask.

"No, I have to stay here. This is where I'm needed most."

"What about Gordon? Can he come, too?"

Doctor Martin answers, "Gordon isn't able to leave these facilities. His history is not... conducive to outside living."

"Homicidal maniac terrorizes post office," explains the cow.

Gordon looks at Pet Shop, and the cow shuts up. Doctor Martin notices how quickly Gordon reacted.

"Doctor MacPherson, has Gordon been more responsive lately?"

"Perhaps a little. Daphne has been spending a lot of time with him, I believe their friendship has opened him up a little."

Doctor Martin frowns. "I hope that's all. We don't want him opening up too much. We should go over his charts later, just to make sure."

Gordon has his fists clenched. He is sweating again. I lean over a little and nudge him, just enough to remind him that I am here. That I care about him. He slowly unclenches his hands.

"Andie, do I have to go? I don't want to be there with a bunch of people I don't know. With nobody who likes me."

"It's only for a couple days, Daphne. And I am sure once they meet you that they will like you. It will be good for you. I know you are strong enough to handle it. Please, do this. For me."

And she has me. Soft, brown eyes full of confidence, full of pride for me, believing in what I could do. Showing trust and concern and love.

I nod, give a quiet "okay" and am rewarded with a big smile and warm squeeze of my hand and that is going to have to be enough to strengthen me for a couple days among strangers.

Fifty-Nine: Final Spin

Gordon and I are sitting on the couch, holding hands. I pull the blanket on top of us, not sure how friendly he wants to get, not sure how friendly I want him to get. But if something happens I would rather have it occur under the covers than out in the open.

Pet Shop is staring as the wheel spins round and round. I am not sure if he even knows what the wheel is for, I think he just likes watching it spin.

I turn to Gordon. "I'm scared of going away. I wish you could come with me."

He gives my hand a squeeze, acknowledging my anxiety. He caresses my cheek with the other hand, brushing back my hair, fingers lingering on the nape of my neck. He is much more Shy Boy turned into Gordon than Scary Gordon clenching fists. Maybe it is just Doctor Martin that makes him like that. I give him my warmest smile, trying to pull him in to kiss me, wanting him to lean down and seal this moment together.

He does lean down, but when I part my lips he angles away from the direct contact. His mouth aims for my ear, and he gives a gentle kiss to it. He holds the position, and I am not certain if this is the most tender way I have ever been kissed or just the silliest.

I hear him breathing against my ear as he holds me. The warm air exhaling, the intake pulling the air back in. It's like a seashell containing all the roar of the ocean, so enormous is the sound of his breathing. And the TV is silent, the hedgehog cannot be heard – all is tuned out save for the rush of his breath across my ear.

The breath slowly, softly, quietly changes. From the toneless in and out variance begins. Bass and treble. White noise turning into coherent sounds. Slowly forming words.

"I love you," Gordon whispers into my ear.

The words echo through the caverns of my mind, increasing in volume until they threaten to shatter my eardrums. It is not Gordon who shouts but my own reaction to them that is making it seem so. His voice, soft so I alone could hear, nevertheless sounds so loud in my mind it drowns all the background noise out.

I pull back, looking fiercely into his eyes. "Gordon, did you..." I leave the question unfinished. The shine in his eyes, the tears falling down his cheek, tell me the answer, let me know it was not my imagination. I hug him tightly, whispering my own love into his ear.

"Lights out," Kareem tells us.

Gordon and I walk to our rooms, hand in hand. I kiss him goodnight, not even caring that we aren't under any covers, that others might see us. He doesn't say anything else, but that's okay. If all he ever says is "I love you," even if he never says it again, I can accept that. I heard it once; I will remember it forever.

Sixty: Midnight Mayhem

I am in a house with a picket fence and a deck in the backyard and a washing machine. I am doing the laundry. I hear the door open and it is Andie, home from work. She looks tired but glad to see me and I give her a kiss and it isn't like an obligation, she isn't kissing me because I keep the house clean, she kisses me because she loves me and I am special to her.

The door opens again and Gordon walks in, home from work. He looks tired but glad to see me and I give him a kiss and it is just like Andie's kiss. I smile at both of them I am so lucky to have the two people I love with me in my nice picket fence house with a kitchen and a stove that I know how to cook on.

Andie and Gordon look at each other and ask each other how work was and they both say fine and they laugh because they asked the same question and answered it the same way. They laugh and then they accidentally bump into each other and then they start kissing.

They tear each other's clothes off and kiss and grab and they don't even see me anymore. They attack each other with a savage passion and soon they are stark naked and stroking each other all over. They fall onto the floor and they start to make love and they are screaming words of ecstasy and telling each other they love one another and I am fading away as they explode in mutual orgasm.

I sit up, sweating, heart racing. A nightmare, I realize, it was just a nightmare. But a new one. This wasn't my past haunting me, it was my own fear of the future. Afraid that the perfect family life isn't an option for me. Frightened that neither Gordon nor Andie will ever be a part of that life with me. Because they can't, or they won't? Because of them, or me?

Minutes become hours as I struggle to fall asleep. It is no use, my mind is racing and my heart is still beating rapidly and I am soaked in sweat. I get up, strip off the sopping clothes. I pull on dry replacements, return to the bed. I freeze when I hear the door open.

His figure looms in the doorframe, silhouetted by the hallway light. At first I fear Sam has come to reattempt his ravage, but then he approaches and I can barely make out Gordon's features in the pale light from the hallway.

He is breathing as hard as I was after the nightmare, his hair is all mussed and his hands are wet when they touch my face. He places a hand on either side of my face and leans in. The kiss is hungry, passionate, animalistic. It is far more demanding than any I have received from him in the past. I sense the need in him, the need to be held, comforted, loved. The need for compassion. The need for union. The need for sex.

Hands still holding my head in place, our kiss continues as he lowers himself onto the bed beside me. I slide my hands under his shirt, they roam his chest, kneading his breasts, fingernails digging into his flesh.

Our lips separate, and even in the near darkness I see his eyes shining. "Daphne," he says softly. I see him struggle to find the words.

"It's okay, Gordon. I know what you want. What you feel. I feel it to. I want to… finish this time."

His eyes are overflowing. His passion, his love, so evident that I can't help crying at the same time I smile with joy.

"Make love to me," I tell him.

He smiles, releasing the hands that had held my head in place during the entire time we had kissed. I lift my own up to latch on to them, to pull them down to my breasts. I bring the interlaced pairs lower in between us and as they are illuminated by the light from the hall I see they are covered in blood and I can't keep myself from screaming at the sight.

"Oh my God, Gordon, what did you do?" I shout, shoving him off of me.

He falls onto the floor, stunned from both my outburst and the sudden change from intimacy to attack. I turn on my room light and am shocked at the sight of him. His hands, arms, clothes – there is blood everywhere. I see the tracks he left on the floor. I look at my own hands and clothes and see the trail of red marks he left.

He rocks on the floor, his arms around his knees, crying. I don't know whether to hold him or run and hide. I look at him, helpless, alone, afraid. As I have been so many times.

I go to him. I reach out, and he clutches me, clinging to my chest, sobbing as a child. I hold him and I rock him until the crying subsides. I lift his head to mine and give him a kiss on the forehead.

"He knew," Gordon says between sobs. "He knew and he was going to make me go away and I wouldn't even know you anymore. Wouldn't love you anymore." His voice gives out, and he just cries in my arms.

"It will be okay, Gordon. Andie will help you. I will help you. We'll all get better together," I promise him. I lie to him. I know what the blood means. I know I will never see Gordon again. I know as soon as they find him it will be Shy Boy forever. Drooling, silent, doorstop Shy Boy. With no light in his eyes, no passion in his soul, no love in his heart.

I pull Gordon up off of the floor. "Let's get you cleaned up," I tell him. I grab some clean sweats and shirts and lead him to the girl's bathroom. I strip the blood-covered clothes off of him and place him under the showerhead. After a second's debate I think what the hell and remove my own, also stained red from our embraces.

I rub the soap all over, cleaning off the red, trying to clean the stain of his deed as well but knowing that is beyond my reach. Even when I wash his genitals, there is no reaction from him. It is a boy not a man who shakes under the hot water. A lost child. I feel ashamed at the way it makes me feel, being there in the shower, naked and wet and covered with suds. I want to reach down and force him hard, to complete the act we began on the bed. But I know that is not what he needs now. That this is about helping Gordon.

I rinse us both off. We step out of the shower. I grab a towel and try to dry him off. It is difficult because he keeps clinging to me. He panics a little whenever he isn't touching me or I am not touching him. I finally get him dry enough to slip a pair of sweats onto him and a t-shirt. He'll have to go commando, I didn't bring any panties and I'm not sure I would want them to find him wearing those anyway.

I hear people running in the hallway. I quickly dress myself. I give him a hug. One last hug. I look him in the eyes. "I love you, Gordon. I'll always love you," I tell him. He says nothing, just looks back at me, as if to burn one last memory in before it is all taken away from him.

Sam comes bursting in. He tackles Gordon, pulling his arm around brutally, shoving a needle into him. I stand silently, tears falling down my cheeks, as the light fades from Gordon's eyes.

Sixty-One: Aftermath

Sixty-One: Aftermath

Andie is here. We sit, side by side, on my bed. The bloodstained sheets are tossed off to the corner of the room. After Sam took Gordon away, I remained in the bathroom until Andie came and brought me back to my room.

"Daphne, I have to ask you some questions."

I nod, understanding she sometimes has to do her job, even when all I want is to hold her and cling to her as Gordon did with me. To have her rock me until my crying subsides. To have her scrub me clean of blood and sin.

"Did you know Gordon was going to attack Doctor Martin?"

I shake my head. "No. I knew he didn't like him. None of us do. He isn't like you, Andie. He is mean and spiteful and doesn't care about any of us."

"Doctor Martin may not be as open as I am," Andie concedes. "But that doesn't make him a bad man. That doesn't justify Gordon's actions."

"I know. Andie, I swear I had no idea that Gordon was going to hurt him. I would have told you."

"I believe you," she says. I wash him clean and she still believes me. I don't deserve this angel, I truly don't.

"I'm more upset at myself, to be honest," Andie says. "I saw the change in Gordon, I knew he was responding more to external situations. I was too optimistic, assuming it was all because he was interacting with people more."

"You mean with me. Did I make him do this?"

"Oh God, Daphne, no!" Andie says, looking shocked at my question. "Don't think that, not even for a minute. It wasn't you. If anybody is to blame, lay it at my feet. I should have checked his charts sooner – I should have realized he wasn't taking his medications."

"You can't be faulted for caring about us, Andie. For treating us as humans. For making us want to become better. If not for you, I never would have left the past. Without your concern, without your guidance, I would still be lost. Surrounded by myself yet still alone. Without you, I never would have found love. Love with Gordon." I hold her hand tighter. "Love with you."

She embraces me. I brush her hair gently with one hand, the other curled around the small of her delicate back. I sit there on the bed, comforting the angel of mercy who has brought me back from the dead. Again I feel my shame as I long to turn the comfort to need, to change the gentle brushes against her hair to aggressive strokes against her body. I push those feelings back, and welcome the compassion, the care, the love that washes over me, engulfing us both as we comfort each other over what we have lost.

Sixty-Two: Reunion

It has been several years since I last visited this cemetery. I kneel beside the weathered tombstone bearing that number I will never forget. Number three seven dash four three three will forever be burned in my mind. But with that number will be the names on this plaque. Norman Jameson, Meredith Booker, Samantha, Zachariah. So many names, remembered by so few. But at least they are known. Known by people like me, who know what lives they lived on this campus.

I trace the many plates on the plaque. My eyes mist when I see the two finely detailed plates that Gordon carved so long ago. I smile when I see Pet Shop's zoo scenes with the dozens of animals. My own drawings look simple, but I think they tell their story well. Even now, I look at them and I feel the connection to the deceased inhabitants of this graveyard. The simple lines etched on metal plates still cry out their message to me. A message of recognition, of personal value, of common bond with humanity. Of love.

My fingers rest on the final plate. My mind travels back, calling forth the memory of its creation.

"Daphne, we've had this conversation a million times. You have to do this. It's an important step in reclaiming your independence."

I look at Andie, pleading, praying, but her resolve does not waver. "But I don't want to be independent. I don't want to be away from here. From you."

Andie sighs. "You don't belong here, Daphne. You have healed. It is time to move on. You need more space, more opportunity to grow. You don't need me anymore."

The words crash down. She says I don't need her but I hear that she doesn't need me. That unless I am broken and bleeding there isn't anything for her to nurse. That she doesn't need me to hold her and to be held by her and to love her and that she will always love me but never be in love with me. Never ever want me the way I want her. Never see a curl of my hair and turn to mush inside like I do when I see that little wisp above her ear.

I call on everyone I have ever had inside me, seeking redemption, seeking salvation from this final decree. But no one is there, it is only me inside, and I realize that I have changed, I am complete, I don't need the others to fill the holes in my being.

I look into those soft brown eyes that have pulled me in so many times. I take my hand and caress her cheek. I think maybe this once, if I ask, she will kiss me.

I don't ask. Instead, my hand falls down. "Okay," I tell her. "I will go."

My last day at Kanapolis Sanitarium is a quiet one. I take Gordon for a walk around the grounds. He is perfect for long, contemplative strolls, always following, never interrupting your train of thought. I wipe the drool off of his chin and kiss him goodbye.

Pet Shop and his menagerie hoot and moo and whistle their goodbyes. "You'll be back," the hedgehog prophesies. Only as a visitor, I think, but I do not dispute his claim out loud.

I even stop by Doctor Martin's office. He is recuperating well. I don't hug him goodbye. Not all is forgiven. But I do thank him for letting Gordon stay where he can be cared for. Where Andie can help him.

Kareem is almost as hard to say goodbye to as Andie will be. I hug him and he lets me give a little kiss. Not on the lips. I ask him if he is gay and he just laughs at me.

Andie. Andie drives me to the bus stop. She presses some money in my hand. I want to give it back but I know I need it and that this last act of love is all I can get from her.

"Thank you, Andie. For believing in me. For making me believe in myself. Thank you for caring about us."

"Daphne, I am so proud of you. I know you will be fine out there. You are strong. You are a wonderful, caring person. I will miss you."

I struggle to hold the tears in. "I'll miss you too. Please take care of Gordon."

"I promise. You'll let me know if you need anything, won't you?"

"I'll be fine," I tell her.

"I know, but still, if you do?"

"If I do, you'll be the first to know."

I hand her the card I made this morning. It isn't as detailed as Gordon's or as pretty as Pet Shop's but it is my final act of acknowledgement to who I have become. She glances at it, looks up and gives me the gift of one last smile. We hug. I regret not stealing a last kiss from her, but think it will be easier on me without that lingering hunger haunting me.

My fingers trace that last plate on the plaque. The names etched on it, Theodore, Glen, Violet, Stuart and Melissa, still visit me in my dreams. But they are most often dreams and not nightmares. They and all the people I met at this place will forever be with me. But they do not control my life now.

I look up from the graveyard, my gaze following the path we trod on so many times, back to the dormitories. I long to follow it again, to see my angel, to see my Andie. To be once more in that presence of beauty, to smell that hair with autumn and crackling fires and holding hands and love all rolled into a sweater and a pleated skirt. To look into those eyes that spoke of hope and promises and rebirth. To taste the sweetness of ambrosia on those lips. To hold the one that I will always love.

"Screech," an owl calls, breaking me out of my reverie. I see him in the big tree, watching me watch my past, and I wonder if he is the same owl we fed toast to. I regret having nothing to toss him.

A final glance along the path, and then I turn the other way. Forward.

www.ingramcontent.com/pod-product-compliance
Lightning Source LLC
Chambersburg PA
CBHW051821170626
46807CB00003B/973